TORTURED BY THE KNIGHT

THE MURDOCH MAFIA SERIES
BOOK 3

SAMANTHA BARRETT

For my Angel baby,
We may never have got to hold you but we sure as hell
loved you.
Your wings may have been ready but our hearts sure as hell
weren't.

AUTHORS NOTE

This book may make some uncomfortable with the content.

I have always sworn if I ever wrote a Mafia book, I would go dark, in order to stay true to my characters and that is what I have done.

Some scenes and descriptions may make you uneasy, make you feel squeamish but rest assured there is an HEA. For those who have read my PNR and thought they were dark, well this is worse, so much worse but in the best way possible.

Welcome to the Murdoch Mafia and all their fucked up shit.

Chapter One

Knight

The taste of nicotine relaxes me. I inhale the smoke, hold it inside me and savor it before blowing it out in a puffy white cloud. I lean against my Dodge and wait for her to come out of the gym. She comes here every day with Allison. Ally was sweet and tender, viewed the world through rose gold glasses until they took her. Koby has been with us for months, her and that pathetic wimp of a brother stay in the guest house.

I know Bishop and King must have a plan but they never include me and Rook—they think we can't stomach this life. I chuckle to myself, if only they knew what I was *really* capable of. The shit I can do makes King's work look like child's play. I'm the quiet brother. I don't need to speak to fill the silence, I relish in it. Rook is the one who laps up the spotlight. I only joined the team at school because he asked me to. Rook wants out of this life—I don't. I want to maim and hurt, I want the blood of my enemies to coat me and watch the life drain from their eyes. I want to hear them beg and scream for their pathetic excuse of a life. I want to break them.

"Stalking again?" I smirk as I slowly turn around and face the Russian bitch. She thinks she's cute sneaking out the back door and trying to catch me off guard. She never will. I heard the gravel crunch under her feet as soon as she rounded the corner. I take in the sight of her. She doesn't wear a sports bra like Ally and Kiara. She wears a loose shirt that hides her shape, her tiny shorts peak out from her under it. Her blonde hair is piled on top of her head and her blue eyes burn with hate. Good, I fucking hate you to!

"Planning to kill my family?" She narrows her eyes and places her hands on her hips.

"I'm not here to hurt your family." I drop my smoke and don't bother to stomp on it as I close the space between us and crowd her until her back is against my car. She doesn't fight me off like I know she could. I push my chest into her, my close proximity doesn't cause her to blush or shudder like most girls, no, Anya Volkov is trained well. I run my nose along the column of her neck causing her to stiffen. Her scent invades my senses and I groan. I may fucking hate her but this Russian bitch gets my cock hard. "You have three seconds to back up or I'll break your fucking jaw." See, I would believe her if I didn't hear the slight hitch in her breathing. I do affect this ice queen after all. I pull back and smirk at the disgusted look that mars her face, then open my mouth to taunt her some more but am cut off.

"You coming, Koby?" I spin around to see Gage standing a few feet away next to his piece of shit car and scowl. The fucker just nods his head at me as Koby brushes past me and stalks toward Gage. I stand here silently fuming that she is fucking going with him! She normally gets a lift home from one of our guys. Where the fuck are they going? Gage starts his car and peels out of the carpark without a backward glance at me. I grind my teeth in frustration and quickly jump in my Dodge and follow them.

I keep a good distance back from them, I don't want to alert Gage to the fact I'm tailing them, I want to see where he plans on taking her. If I find out he is a rat and helping her in any way to take my family down, I'll put a bullet in his fucking skull myself. He and Koby spend the most time together. Ally trains with her but never stays as late as Koby. Her brother stays in the guest house and never leaves. Something is up with these two and I want to know what it is and why the fuck they have hidden their true identities. Allison swears she had no idea who they really are, she thought they were just kids who knew about the bratva. My brothers, Kiara and Ally are the only ones who know about their little secret. We have allowed them to stay with us still —keep your friends close but your enemies closer and all that shit.

Gage takes a right, heading toward skid row. What the fuck are they doing down here? I keep back and wait to see if he's passing through or not, he pulls his car into an alleyway of sorts. I grit my teeth as I have to park my baby on the street. All the bums' eyes light up at the sight of her. I get out and shoot each of them a scathing look before grabbing my phone from my pocket and dialing Mav's number, he answers on the second ring.

"Knight?"

"Track my car's GPS and have someone come watch it. Anything happens to it and I'm coming for you." I end the call and fucking pray for Mav's sake someone gets here in time to stop her from being stripped and burnt out. I follow after Gage and Koby and make sure to stick to the shadows. I don't want them to make me or all this will be for nothing. It pisses me off that I had to call Mav, I don't know what it is but that guy really rubs me the wrong fucking way. He's too good. I'm not a jealous guy or anything like that but mark my words, Mav is hiding something and I'm going to find out what it is as soon as I deal with my Russian problem. Gage keeps moving with ease and I can tell this isn't his first time here. Watching how sure footed Koby is in the dark lets me know she has been here before as well. I have no idea what the fuck could be out in this part of town but I'm about to find out as Gage yanks open a tiny side door. I flatten against the side of a building and wait a few moments before following after them.

I yank the door open and furrow my brow, it's a corridor! I keep walking and spot another door at the end. I push it open and I'm immediately assaulted by the base of the music and lights flashing that blind me for a moment. I scour the area, there must be a thousand people in here. I lift the hood of my sweatshirt up to try conceal my identity,

I don't need these fuckers recognizing me. I shoulder my way through the crowd and down a flight of stairs. The smell in this place is sickening—sweat, blood, rank body odor, you name the most rancid smell you can think of and that is what this place smells like. As I push through the crowd to get a better look at what has them congregated, I cop an elbow to the ribs. It takes everything inside me not to pull my gun and plant a bullet in the fucker's head. I glare at the drugged-out son of a bitch, and whatever he sees in my eyes has him backing down, raising his hands in surrender. I don't break eye contact with the piece of shit until he disappears into the crowd. At the sound of cheers, I spin around and push my way through the crowded area, then slam to a stop at the sight in front of me.

What in the seven fucking hells!

Koby stands off to one side of the circle in the middle of the crowd. Gone is her baggy shirt as she stands here bouncing on the balls of her feet. Her hands are taped and she now wears a pair of black tights and a black sports bra, along with a white mouth guard which gleams under the lighting. Gage stands beside her, saying some shit into her ear. She cracks her neck side to side. I follow her line of sight and my eyes widen in surprise—she's having an underground fight.

Chapter Two

Koby

Adrenaline courses through me as I eye my opponent. She's lean and smaller than me but I won't be making the mistake of underestimating her because of her size. This bitch has a rep around these parts. She is known to be dirty which Gage and I have been preparing for. She won't catch me off guard, I need the prize money from this fight. If I keep up this streak, that means I'm one step closer to getting me and Dimitri the fuck out. He isn't built for this life and I am the only person who gives a fuck about him. I planned this shit out perfectly and I got us the protection we need. He will never find us here, not in the midst of his enemy—it is the last place he would think to look for us.

"Don't fuck around." I clear my mind and focus on

what Gage is saying. "You strike first. She favors her left side and I think her ribs are still bruised from the fight a couple weeks back. Go for the left and put her down quick. She has a longer reach than you, so watch for that." I check out her left side and can still see some bruising marring the side of her body. I don't like exploiting weak points but I also don't want to lose—I need the 5k prize this fight offers. "You have three rounds. I want her down by the end of the first!" I turn my head and stare at him. He has to be joking but the look on his face tells me he is dead serious.

"Do you know how hard that will be?" It's fucking hard talk with my mouth guard in but Gage insists that if I don't wear it, I don't fight!

"Do it, Koby. I don't want to get caught. Knight has been following you everywhere and we can't let him find out about this!" At the mention of the middle Murdoch child, my body begins to thrum with awareness. The sight of him angers me but at the same time the haunted look in his dark brown eyes makes me want to fight his demons. I want to take away his pain. I shake that stupid thought away. He and his family are a means to an end and that's it.

"Okay." Our unofficial ref enters the circle. Gage gives me one last pat on the shoulder before gripping my face between his hands and leaning his forehead against mine. This has become our *thing*—before each fight he always does this and it centers me, keeps me humble and in the moment instead of getting caught up in my own head.

"You got this, babe. Knock her out and take the win, then we can celebrate." I close my eyes and nod, take a couple deep breaths before he lets go and slinks back into the crowd. I move to the center when the ref calls us in.

Claudia—my opponent—stands at least a foot taller than me. I crane my neck back and hold her gaze as the ref runs through the rules.

"The only rule, there is no rules!" The crowd roars around us. I'm not a cocky bitch and try to intimidate her. I just hold her gaze and wait for the ref to push us back. What does catch my attention though is the fact she is wearing gloves. I turn to look at Gage over my shoulder and ask him about it but the ref calls fight and the bitch strikes me while I'm not looking. I stumble into the crowd and they push me back. My vision is fuzzy and the side of my temple where she hit is pounding. I growl in annoyance. Claudia has a cocky grin on her face—the ugly bitch has brass knuckles on under those fucking gloves!

"Kill her!"

"Claudia for the win!" The crowd shouts around me. Their doubt in me just fuels my rage as I circle around and wait for her to attack. Then she does. She strikes out with a right hook and I duck swinging out with my left to connect with her ribs. she curls over and stumbles back a step, I don't stop. I launch at her. she's backed against the crowd and these blood-hungry cunts won't allow her to slip by them so I wail on her. Punch after punch to the face and I land a few good hooks to ribs that I feel them crack under my knuckles and wish I didn't feel bad... but she cheated! Her eyes roll backward as I land another blow, her team throws in a white towel. The ref yanks me back and the crowd boos. I smile and turn toward Gage ready to run and hug him when I'm hit from behind. The force of the hit sends me to my knees and has my vision swimming with black dots. The noise around me grows quiet and I sway side to side. Gage drops to his knees in front of me and cups my face. I feel some sort of liquid dripping down the back of my neck. Gage darts his gaze over my head and I panic when his eyes widen, he grips me and turns me so my back is to his chest.

I lazily look up, still dazed from the hit. I blink my eyes a couple times to try and get my eyes to focus... I see Knight standing there with his gun pressed against Claudia's fore-head. I can tell it's him because he wears the same clothes from earlier. The color drains from her face, as two men step forward and look as if they are ready to lay into Knight. I spit my mouth guard and plead to Gage.

"You need to help him." Even my voice sounds drunk, she must have got me good.

"Nah, babe, he's got this." The two men stand either side of Claudia. One wears a pair of brass knuckles as well. The music and the roar of the crowd has died down, it's so quiet in here that my ears ring from the shock of it.

"You got one chance here, boy—" Knight laughs and pushes his hood back. When both men recognize who he is they instantly take a step back and their faces grow slack. Knight rams the barrel of the gun into her head harder as he speaks.

"You dirty shot her." Claudia keeps her lips pressed together. I can tell from the look in her eyes that she is in pain. Knight is stiff and coiled with rage, no one around us will dare move against him or say a thing because they know exactly who he is. He doesn't need an entourage or men surrounding him. He may be the quiet one from what I have noticed, but he is just as deadly as his two older brothers. "You and your family are done in this town." Claudia's eyes widen in fear, all her bravado from earlier is gone and replaced by horror.

"I-I didn't know she was with you."

"Well now you do. You have till sunrise to be gone." Gasps ring out around us. He drops his gun back to his side and turns his back to her, effectively dismissing her without remorse. He stares down at Gage and I for a moment, his brown eyes are filled with anger. "Can you walk?" I push forward from Gage but only end up slumping back against him, my vision swims and I know I'm about to pass the fuck out.

Knight

I grind my teeth as I shove my gun into the back of my pants, ignoring all the stares on me as I lean down and grab her—Gage doesn't fight me—lift her bride style in my arms and turn to head out. The crowd parts for me now they know who I am. Gage is hot on my heels as I make my way out of the run-down building. Koby is limp in my arms and I can feel her blood seeping through my sweatshirt. Grinding my teeth in anger, I fight the urge to turn back and kill the bitch who dared to hurt her. Gage pushes past me and opens the door to the corridor, then runs to the next one and pushes it open. We exit the building without a word being spoke. He's smart enough to know that if he speaks right now, he'll wear the brunt of my rage.

My dodge comes into view and I sigh with relief at the sight of her not being damaged. Mav leans against my car. I narrow my eyes at him and the fucker just smirks. He's too comfortable and it grates on my frayed nerves that he thinks he isn't replaceable.

"Move!" I snap at him. He shifts out of the way and I have to balance Koby in my arms in order to retrieve my keys and open the door. I place her in the passenger's seat and buckle her in, then step back and run my gaze over her looking for any other injuries; but there are none to be found. I close the door and turn back to face Mav and Gage. Only one of them looks worried and he fucking should be. There is no way Bishop sanctioned Gage to fight Koby in that pit of a place. "Meet me at home," is all I say to Gage as I round the car and hop in.

The whole way back I have kept checking on her to make sure she is okay. She took a hard hit to the head and I know it's wrong to let her sleep but it's not like I had a choice when she passed the fuck out in Gage's hold. I park the car in front of the house and groan when I see lights still on inside—of course fucking Mav called Bishop about what went down. I climb out and move around to her side, lift her from the car and she cuddles into my chest. I glare at the blood that coats my seat. She needs a fucking doctor! I carry her up the stairs and do the thing I swore I wouldn't, I bring the enemy into my family's home. Bishop, King, Ally, Kiara and Rook all stand there. The girls look horrified at the sight, while my brothers show nothing.

"What happened?" Ally rushes to ask as she comes forward and checks her friend. I keep my gaze on Bishop as I say,

"She needs a doctor. She took a blow to the back of the head and it hasn't stopped bleeding." Bishop eyes me warily for a moment, he has every right to. I have done nothing but fight him at every turn for having Koby and her brother here. Now here I am asking him to help her. He pulls his phone from his pocket and dials a number before placing it against his ear.

"Get a doctor here now." He steps aside and motions for me to come forward. I've just taken a single step when I hear a car door slam. King and Bishop pull their guns, I shake my head knowing exactly who it is.

"It's just Gage." Again, Bishop eyes me like I've grown a fucking second head. Him, King and Rook may be accepting of Gage, but he hasn't done shit to show me that I can trust his ass! I lay Koby down gently on the couch, and cringe when I see her blood coating my forearm. I grit my teeth trying to quell the rage inside me. I want to fucking destroy her not watch some other assholes do it for me. Her pain and misery will be by my hands not someone else's. I stand here and stare down at her. How can someone so fucking vile look so innocent?

"What happened?" Ally asks as she kneels down beside her friend and runs the back of her hand over her cheek.

"She was hit from behind," I answer.

"By fucking who?" King growls. I dart my gaze to Gage as he walks through the door. The fucker doesn't even look worried that he has just walked into the lion's den. He may be Tony's bastard and related to us by blood but that doesn't mean shit to me.

"Ask that bastard. He's the one who set up her fight at Chop's Den." Bishop and King both swing toward Gage. Kiara's eyes widen, she knows exactly what fighting at Chop's Den entails. Bishop steps toward Gage, but Kiara darts out in front of him with her back to Gage and stares at Bishop with a pleading look in his eyes.

"Bish, please don't hurt him." Gage reaches out and places a hand on Kiara's shoulder. She shrugs it off and still tries to defend him against my brother. "Bishop, don't!"

Bishop tenses and I can tell he is debating what to do. The lover in him wants to listen to his fiancée but the Don also knows he cannot let this go unpunished.

"Princess, he knew what would happen. He went against the rules and defied the boss—"

Kiara glares at King and shakes her head. "No. There is no way Koby wasn't willing to fight."

"She's right." I drop my gaze back to the blonde who has taken up way too much of my head space lately. She flinches as she pushes herself up into a sitting position. Allison tries to help but Koby waves her off, her green eyes lifting to mine.

"Can you step back so I can stand?" I keep my face blank and stay where I am for a moment until her eyes pinch at the corner showing her pain. I find myself extending a hand toward her. She eyes it warily for a beat before placing her taped hand in mine.

I look down at her. I can see the fire in her eyes and it calls to the beast inside me. This girl is the enemy and yet I find myself wanting to make sure she is okay and remains unharmed. I need to put distance between us, the problem with that is I've been doing it since she moved in here and Gage has swept in. I've seen the way he is with her, how he can get her to smile easily and the way she trusts him. She brushes past me and moves toward my brothers, each of them eye her warily but don't say a word.

"How you doing, killer?" I grind my teeth in anger and manage to keep my retort inside at Gage's question.

She shrugs her shoulders, "I'm okay, we won so that's all that matters."

Gage stuffs his hands in his pockets and rocks back on his heels, clearly feeling awkward. Koby releases a sigh as she turns to Bish, he eyes her with the same distrust I do.

"It was my idea," she says firmly. Bishop cocks a single brow at her as he answers.

"What was?"

"The fight. It was my idea, not Gage's. If you want to punish someone then you punish me. I'll take whatever you throw at me, big man." Bishop's face remains impassive as he stares down at Koby. Gage moves slightly so he is standing in front of Koby, shielding her.

"Who told you about the fight?" King asks.

"I did," Gage answers.

Koby scoffs. "Bullshit. One of the fighters at the shack told me about it." Gage tries to cut in but Koby pushes on. "G said not to do it but I wouldn't listen. I don't conform to the same rules as your family." Bishop's gaze darkens and I find myself moving forward ready to stop Bish if he lashes out. Ally moves to stand by King and Kiara tries to gain

Bishop's attention, but he's in Don mode and won't be distracted by anything.

Bish flicks his gaze to me. "You knew about her fighting?" I cut my gaze to Koby as I answer Bish.

"Yeah, I told Gage to set it up."

Chapter Four

Koby

What the hell?

Knight stands here staring at me while lying to his brother. He had no fucking idea about the fights! I can see the anger in his eyes, it's like they darken the longer he stares at me. All I need is the money from this fight and two more then I can go. I will never have to see them again. Dimitri and I will finally be free and *their* sacrifice will be worth it.

"Bullshit!" King snarls as he turns to his younger brother. "Don't fucking lie to cover either of their asses." Knight's face remains void of emotion as he slowly looks to King.

"I'm not lying. I wanted her to get her ass beat." I hear Kiara snort beside me.

"Knight, there is no way you wanted that." It annoys me that Kiara speaks as if she knows Knight well. Allison has told me they grew up together. I can see from the way he shields himself from the others that no one really knows the *real* Knight. He allows his family to see what he wants them to but nothing more.

"How can you be so sure, Kiara?" The bite in his tone is clear. I hear Bishop grunt behind me in disapproval.

"Because if you wanted her hurt, you would have left her there and not brought her back." I stare at Knight, slightly taken back by Kiara's words. His eyes narrow on me.

"That's because if anyone is going to kill her, it's going to be me!" He storms out of the room without another word. I'm not used to caring about someone other than Dimitri, so the feelings I have toward Knight scare the shit out of me. He thinks I don't know that he lurks in the woods by the guest house or that he follows me wherever I go. I was trained from the age of two to fight and kill. I know how to track and I also know how to spot a tail. This mafia heir needs to learn a few things if he wishes to catch me by surprise.

"Go back to the guest house, the doctor will see you there." I turn back to Bishop and narrow my eyes.

"I don't need a doctor," I grit out before turning to Gage. "Walk me back." It isn't a question. Gage follows without argument, neither of us speak a word until we are away from the house and half way across the yard. The living room light is on inside the guest house. Dimitri leaves it on for me when he goes to bed. A whoosh of air escapes me, I don't know what Anya was thinking sending Dimitri with me. I'm so tired of all the lies and the secrets. I speak so many lies that I don't even know how to tell the truth anymore. I know the Murdoch's think they know who I am but they honestly have no fucking idea. I'm not someone special or even someone worth their time. I'm only here because I need to keep Dimitri safe. It's a vow I swore and I will never break it.

"Want to tell me what's going on between you and the dark Knight?" I stop walking and face Gage. I won't lie, he is ruggedly handsome and a really good guy. From what I have seen he is good friends with both Allison and Kiara. He offered to train Dimitri as well. D isn't like us, he doesn't deal well with crowds or… people in general.

"There is nothing going on—" The dry stare Gage gives me has me clamping my mouth shut.

"I've known Knight a while. I've known all of these assholes a long time."

I roll my eyes. "That's because they are your brothers!"

"That isn't the reason, Koby. I'm the bastard of this family. The only people who know my relationship to them are all here. Did you think just because my asshole daddy is rich that I got to go to private schools and not have a care in the world?" He doesn't give me a chance to answer. "I fought for every fucking thing I have. Some stupid ass part of me can't seem to walk away from the assholes though." I hear the anguish in his voice. I reach out and grip his hand in mine. I'm not used to comforting people, I never really have, so I hope I'm doing it right.

"You're a good guy, that's why you stay. Hell, you're the only person here, aside from Kiara and Ally, that is actually nice to me. I like you so that has to count." A small smile tugs at the corners of his mouth. He waggles his brows at me causing a groan of annoyance to slip free of my lips.

"You *like* like me, don't ya, babe?" I close my eyes and lean my head back to pray to whoever the fuck is listening to give me strength.

"You fucking him?" At the sound of his angry voice I stand straighter and look directly at him. Knight stands there shrouded in the darkness of the bushes glaring at me.

"Bro, it isn't like that—" Knight cuts his angry glare to Gage, silencing him.

"Get the fuck out of here now." Gage turns to me, the look he gives tells me if I say no, he will stay and weather whatever punishment follows from Knight.

"You should go, he won't do anything." I ignore the growl that comes from Knight as I focus on Gage. He nods and squeezes my hand before letting it go.

"You need anything just call." I nod my thanks and watch him walk away. The pounding in my head intensifies as I turn back to face Knight. He moves out of the shadows and stalks toward me. His eyes blaze with rage sending a shiver of dread down my spine. He doesn't stop until there is but a sliver of space between us. I have to crane my head back to meet his gaze, his chest rising and falling in rapid pants.

"You're not fucking calling him!" he grits out through clenched teeth. I'm too tired and in way too much pain to hash this argument out with him.

"Okay," is all I say as I turn and head toward the guest house. I close and lock the door behind me heading straight for the bathroom that is attached to the room I stay in. I turn the faucet on and strip off my clothes, dumping them in the hamper before stepping under the spray. A hiss escapes me as the water hits the cut on the back of my head. I look down at the drain and cringe when I see the water is tinted red from my blood. I grab some shampoo and gently rub it into my hair gritting my teeth through the sting, that fucking bitch blind shot me!

Once I finish washing myself I step out of the shower and wrap my long hair in a towel before drying my body with another. Wrapping the towel around myself I head into my room and freeze at the sight of Knight sitting on the end of my bed. His forearms rest on the tops of his thighs, his head is hung low with his hood up shielding his face from me.

I decide to ignore his presence as I head to the dresser that holds my minimal belongings. I grab out a crop top and pair of sleep shorts. I pull the shorts on under my towel then keep my back to him as I drop the towel and pull the crop top on. I grab my brush off the dresser and gently try to comb out the knots without aggravating the cut any further. A head knock fucking sucks, that's for sure. A hiss escapes me when I snag a large knot. Before I can move an inch, I'm spun around hitting my back against the dresser with Knight caging me in with his body. Done with his manly display I scowl up at him and snap.

"What the fuck is your problem? I haven't done anything to you and yet here you are trying to make a problem when there isn't one."

"You're hurt!" His statement shocks me silent for a moment.

"And?" I query. He ignores my question as he grips my

hand and leads me back into the bathroom. He grips my hips, then lifts me so I'm sitting on the vanity. My body tenses as he grips the back of my neck and pushes my head down to inspect the damage. I bite my cheek to keep from lashing out at him, my fists clenched at my sides ready to fight if I need to. He pushes my hair out of his way, surprisingly gentle as he gets closer to the cut.

"You need stitches." I push his hands away and straighten. He moves between my spread legs closing the space between us. He is still a few inches taller than me.

"I'm not getting stitches."

His eyes narrow. "You can either get them willingly or I'll have the doc knock you out and do it anyway."

"What? You're not gonna do the honors and knock me out yourself?" He grinds his teeth in annoyance.

"I would never lay a hand on you, Koby. I may not like you or even be able to stomach the sight of you but that still doesn't mean I would ever lay a hand on you." I can hear the truth in his words... It's so strange to hear a male vow to never lay hands on a woman.

"All I've known since the day I was born is that the male race is superior to the female. Where I come from men can do as they like to women and never be held accountable." His eyes darken at my admission.

"That's not how shit works around here!" he growls. Call me stupid but I believe that Knight would never physically harm me. I try to push him back so I can climb off the counter but he shoots his arms out and leans forward, forcing me to lean back against the mirror. We're eye to eye —I can see the demons that haunt him in his gaze, they speak to the ones inside me.

"What happened to you?" The words fly out of my mouth before I can stop them. He immediately pulls back. I find I am able to breathe easier with the space he has put between us.

"None of your fucking business. Let's go."

"Where?"

His eyes narrow. "I told you the doc is going to stitch up that mess." He turns and leaves while I glare at the bastard. If he thinks I'll follow after him he has another thing coming!

Chapter Five

Knight

"Put me down now before I gut you like a fucking pig!" She punches my back and tries to wiggle free of my hold. I grit my teeth. The little shit packs a good hit. She refused to come willingly so I was forced to take action. She's now over my shoulder and spewing threats at me as I take her back to the main house where the doc waits. I tire of her hits and fucking insults so I smack her ass hard enough leaving my palm stinging, making her yelp in surprise. "Did you just fucking smack me?" The disbelief in her voice is comical.

"Yeah, I fucking did. Keep wriggling and talking shit, I'll do it again!" I feel her tense but she does as instructed and remains still but not silent!

"My head is pounding, can I walk?" *Fuck!* I stop in the

middle of the lawn near the main house. I forgot all about her head when I threw her over my shoulder kicking and screaming—literally.

"What's the magic word?"

"Are you fucking kidding me?" she shouts. I bite my bottom lip to stop my smile from breaking free.

"I never joke around," I say in a flat tone.

"Well maybe you should!" She remains silent for a second before her body goes slack. "Knight, can you put me down... *please?*" I slowly pull her from my shoulder and place her on her feet, gripping her waist as she sways slightly. She's flush against my front. Her eyes slowly lift to mine and I see the darkness in her gaze that she tries to hide.

Unlike the others I live and bathe in darkness, my black soul calls to hers.

"Was that so hard?" She narrows her eyes and lifts her upper lip in a snarl.

"Yes, yes it fucking was!" she snaps before yanking free of my hold and storming toward the house.

I lay in my bed staring up at the ceiling. After the doc stitched Koby, Allison walked her back to the guest house. It's been hours and still I can't sleep. Every fucking time I close my eyes, all I see is the anguish and betrayal in King's eyes. I never knew Mela was King's the night I met Christine. If I had known, I would never have let her leave. That fucked-up bitch used me. She fucked with my head so bad, making me believe that we were in love. I was just a fucking kid and didn't know any better, all I knew was she could make me hard and then make me feel good.

King won't even look at me the same now and I don't blame him. I stabbed my brother in the back, all for some psycho bitch who made me think I was in love. I vowed to myself the night Christine drove away from me that I would never love again. I would never let another female hold any power over me. My guilt eats at me daily and it's why I pour so much time in Amelia. I want to right my wrongs but I don't fucking know how! I've always been the quiet reserved twin. Rook is outgoing and the life of any party. Sometimes... I wish I could be more like him. People take one look at me and back away. It's like they can see the devil in my eyes and know I'm pure darkness.

Koby is the first person to look at me with something other than fear, she isn't scared of me or worried I might hurt her. She baits me and taunts me to unleash on her, I don't know if she does it consciously or not. Each time I'm around her and I feel gravity trying to pull me to her, I tell myself it's because she is Russian scum. Truthfully, if she's scum, then I'm trash. I need to earn my brother's respect back. If I have to take down the first girl to make me feel something other than disgust since Christine, I'll do it. Bishop took King's hate when he thought Bish was the one to kill his ex. He did it for me. Bishop pieced it all together that night when I got home and he saw how broken I was. I never confirmed his suspicion, but that's the thing with Bishop, he takes one look at you and he just knows. I guess that's his superpower and mine is fucking everything up.

I growl in frustration and decide to give up on sleep since I barely fucking sleep anyway. Unlike my twin who can sleep through a fucking bomb, I only sleep an hour or two a night and then survive on coffee and energy drinks. I wander downstairs to get something to drink, preferably some of Bishop's good fucking whiskey. I head straight for Bishop's office to raid his stash but pause when I hear him and King talking.

"We have to make a move, they are getting too close." I can hear the frustration in King's voice which makes me uneasy, King doesn't rattle easily.

"We can't make a move now. Pauly and Vinny know we are coming for them!" Bishop sounds stressed and he never shows emotion, so hearing him now has the hairs on the back of my neck rising.

"Bish, we need to——" I hear a fist slam down on the desk silencing King.

"I fucking know! We have so much more to fucking lose now, don't you see that? It's not just us anymore, King. We have the twins, Kiara, Ally and Mela. They will be used against us. I will not let Kiara be used again!"

"You think I want Allison to be fucking hurt? Or my daughter? I want this finished so that the girls and the twins can live a life we were never granted. I see the demons of Knight's past in his eyes." I suck in a sharp intake of air at the mention of my name. "He is drowning, Bishop, and I don't know how to fucking help him."

"I've been trying for years, King. Knight hides in the shadows while Rook buries himself in anything with a hole and uses humor as a mask. Knight needs your forgiveness——"

"How the fuck can I do that, Bishop? Every time I look at him all I see is him betraying me. He was sleeping with her, Bishop... he knew about Amelia!" Shame washes over me and I drop my head.

"He was a fucking kid that she manipulated. It wasn't his fucking fault! He had no idea that Christine was pregnant with *your* child. He is the best hacker we have. He thinks I don't know about his extracurricular activities. I know he is the one who is blocking Luka from being able to find more information on Koby and Dimitri. He is closing us out and pulling away, King. He doesn't even spend time with Meelz anymore. I won't lose another member of this family." That piques my interest.

"We haven' lost Car, Bish. She just needed a... break." I hear Bishop sigh.

"She needed a break because I failed her. It's my fault we lost our sister. I should have known what Tony was doing to them both, but I was too caught up in my own shit." I clench my hands into fists at my sides, the reminder of what that sick piece of shit did to Kiara and Carlina makes me sick to my stomach. What kind of fucking person does that to a child? Fucking hell, Car was only a couple years older than Amelia when Tony started fucking with her.

"Carlina will come back. Until then, we need to focus on keeping the twins safe and the girls guarded at all times." I hear Bish snort.

"How the fuck are we going to keep Knight here? Rook will do as he is told if it means he gets a new car." I smirk, they're not wrong. My twin will do anything you ask if it means he gets a new car, hence the fucker already has four!

"Simple." The way King says that one word has my hackles raising, his tone is cold and detached. "You keep the

Russian here and Knight will stay." I grind my teeth, the fucker thinks he knows me but he doesn't.

"I need him to get close to her, he's been the only person she has let her guard down around." Bishop catches me by surprise. "I just need the information from her. Rook hasn't heard from Car again and that leaves us with Knight—"

"He's too risky, we can't count on him to get the job done." Having heard enough, I walk into Bishop's office. Both of them stand and stare at me in surprise. I keep my face blank as I look only at Bishop and ignore King.

"I'll get you your information." Bish's eyes widen slightly. "When I get you what you want," I look to King as I finish, "I want my freedom from this family. You won't track me like you do Car. I want out!" I don't wait for a reply, but stalk out of the room and make my way to the guest house. Koby may not know it yet but she will give me everything I need so I can get the fuck out of here and stop being the families fuck-up. I can't stay here with King and Bishop. Bishop tries to hide his emotions but I can tell this thing with me and King is killing him. I won't be the reason King can't relax. He is always on edge when I'm around Ally or Mela and I don't want that. I want him to feel comfortable with the girls roaming the house and not worried I'm going to fuck his girl.

Chapter Six

Koby

He may think he moves silently but I heard the moment he opened the front door. Instead of greeting him with a fist to the face, I decided to lay here and see what he would do. I mean, I do have a gun tucked under my pillow and my switch blade under the side of the mattress. I keep my eyes closed and allow my other senses to take over as my bedroom opens. I hear him padding across the carpet. The mattress dips on the other side, I make sure to relax my body and face void of expression so I can keep feigning sleep. I expect him to lash out, or shake me awake, what I don't fucking expect is to feel his lips against mine!

My eyes snap open, ready to shove him away, but when I meet his brown eyes and see the uncertainty in his gaze, I freeze. He pulls back slowly and stares down at me. I stay stock still as I gaze up at him waiting for him to explain what the fuck just happened. He opens and closes his mouth twice before he slips off the bed and heads for the door. I watch in stunned silence as he walks out without so much as a backward glance.

What the fuck just happened?

Rather than sit here and spend hours wondering, I launch from the bed and chase after him, I catch up when he is halfway across the lawn. I call out but he doesn't stop, so I cut him off by standing in front of him. He glares down at me. I huff out my annoyance—he came in and kissed *me*, not the other way around, so why the hell is he pissy?

"Move," he grinds out.

I place my hands on my hips and scowl up at him. "Get real, I'm not moving until you tell me what the hell *that* was!" He bends so we are eye level, the heat of his breath fans across my face.

"That was a mistake." I make sure to keep the shock from my face, shove against his chest but he doesn't budge. He grips my wrist in one of his hands and spins me so my back is flush against his chest. I don't fight him, I want to see what he is going to do next. He runs his nose down the column of my neck, making a shiver roll through me. How Knight Murdoch can pull this type of reaction from my body I'll never understand. His free hand runs across my chest electing a small gasp from me until he grips my throat.

"I'll kill you before you try anything." He chuckles and buries his face in the crook of my neck. The grip he has on my throat doesn't tighten.

"I would love to see you try, *Anya*." Everything inside

me freezes. I stiffen in his hold as my mind reels. He just called me *Anya*! How the fuck does he know about her? No one knows about Anya and what we did to get here. I will not let Knight derail the plan I have in place to get us the fuck out of this. I keep my lips shut and say nothing, he can think what he likes but he'll never know the truth, I'll die before anyone finds out.

"Get your hands off me," I grit out through clenched teeth. He releases me and I put a couple of feet of space between us, slam my mask back in place and watch as he does the same.

"Whatever you have planned, just know I will sabotage you. You will not take my family down."

"You have no fucking idea what you are talking about. You are fucking pathetic and it is comical how you think you have the upper hand." His upper lip pulls back in a snarl.

"I know that you are a *rata* and are nothing more than a bitch trying to prove herself to her daddy. Let me tell you something, little girl." He closes the space between us and I crane my neck back to keep eye contact. "You fuck with my family and I'll show you a side of me not many have seen. King may be the one Bishop calls on for *extraction* but, unlike him, I love getting bloody and listening to my victims scream. It makes me rock fucking hard." I grind my teeth so hard I fear I may break them. He shoulders past me, heading toward his house while I stand here trying to tamper my rage.

"You shouldn't be here." I glare at Gage's back as he lands blow after blow to the punching bag. The man is good. Without even turning he knew I was here, his senses are about as good as mine.

"Why not?" I ask as I drop my bag on the bench seat and move toward him to hold the bag. He runs his gaze over me as I grip the bag, but says nothing. He doesn't pull his punches or worry that the force of the landing on the bag will knock me down. He respects me and I appreciate that. He knows I can hold my own and don't need to be babied like the others. "Does Kiara fight?" That gets him to pause and focus on me.

"Why?" I can hear the suspicion in his voice. I've let this family think I know nothing about them, when in truth, I know they have a sister and Gage is their half-brother. I know more about this family and their dealings than their inside men. I didn't get to where I am today by being docile. Everything they perceive about me is an act.

"I'm just curious," I say with a shrug. He shakes his head as he backs up.

"If you think Bishop will let her in the ring with you, you're out of your fucking mind." I roll my lips over my teeth and nod. I figured as much. "Why do you want to fight her?" The way he tenses tells me he is starting wonder if everything the others say about me is true. Gage is a lot of things but he isn't dumb. He knows there is more to me than meets the eye. He may be the only Murdoch to see beneath my mask.

"I heard she is undefeated and wanted to change that." His eyes widen and a huge smile splits across his face.

"You won't be able to get a paid match with her but I

can set one up here." He nods his head toward the training ring and I grin. Fighting Kiara doesn't have anything to do with my plan, this fight is all for me.

I spend the next few hours training with Gage. I love the way my muscles burn after a good training session with him. Just because I'm no longer in Russia doesn't mean I can slack off. I need to keep up my training in case they come looking. I head for the showers and make quick work of undressing. No one is in here at this time. I turn the shower on and step under the spray. The cold water eases some of the tension in my body. I don't know how people can stand to be under the hot spray. I've always preferred cold to hot. I lather the shampoo through my hair and freeze when I feel a presence. I turn the shower off and grab my towel. Wrapping it around my body I turn left toward the lockers and pause as I strain my hearing.

Nothing.

Just as I talk myself into believing the feeling I had was all in my head, I hear movement behind me. Spinning I strike out. Knight dodges the hit and I growl. He stands here in a pair of blue jeans and a gray sweatshirt with the hood up. His dark eyes bore into mine, as I'm standing here in nothing but a towel with shampoo still in my hair.

"What the hell are you doing here?" I snap at him.

"Just checking in on the Russian spy." The disgust in his voice is apparent. I ignore it.

"Well, as you can see, I'm standing here holding a private meeting with the Bratva conspiring to take down your family." His upper lip lifts in a snarl as I spread my feet apart to be ready in case he decides to come at me.

"You think you are so smart. You are nothing!"

"Good to know. Now if you would kindly fuck off," I sneer at him whilst shouldering past. I ignore him all together as I drop my towel and head for the shower, again. I close my eyes to rinse my hair. He may think he has me in a vulnerable position but he is a fool. I'll hear him, feel him if he moves a step closer to me and it will be his worst mistake if he thinks he can take me down.

Chapter Seven

Knight

Her body is sculpted to perfection, every part molded perfectly. I follow the suds from the shampoo as it flows down her body. Her tits are perky and pebbled from the cold spray. The suds roll down the crease between her tits and continue down her flat, toned stomach. I give up following it as it rolls straight past her pussy. Fuck! The sight of her bare pussy has my mouth watering for a taste of her, my cock straining inside my pants. I bite my lip to stop the groan that wants to break free when she runs her hands down her body. She does it innocently and has no idea the effect that is having on me.

Leaning against the wall, I watch as she conditions her hair and runs her fingers through it to get rid of all the knots.

I swallow a few times trying to get my body on board with my mind—we hate her! She is a means to an end, getting the information from her about the Russian's means I can leave. My family won't be divided with me gone. They will be able to go back to being happy with no tension or worrying about me—the dark one of the family. I'm the unstable one they fear, they think if I'm pushed too hard I'll snap. They aren't wrong, there is a darkness inside me that is only quieted whenever *she* seems to be around. What they all don't know is, I fight as well.

I've been fighting for years, I needed an outlet for my rage and thirst for blood. Bishop won't allow me to get involved in what King does. What he doesn't know is Mav brings some of those assholes to me instead of King. Mav is just as fucked up as I am, he loves to paint the walls with our enemy's blood and laugh in their faces as they scream. I refocus on her when she shuts the water off, then squeezes her hair to rid it of excess water before gripping her towel and wrapping it around her delectable body. I glare at the white fucking towel that blocks my view of her. Her chuckle has me snapping my gaze to hers and narrowing my eyes.

"Like what you see, playboy?" I don't answer, I just stand here and watch as she heads to her locker and begins to dress. I nearly choke on my tongue when she bends over giving me a full view of her ass and pussy as she slips her pink lace... thong on.

Fuck!

Just seeing her in nothing but that thin scrap of lace has my cock ragging harder and wanting to be buried deep inside her. I hate to admit it, but it takes a lot more strength than I want to admit to remove my gaze from her. I'm here for a purpose and that doesn't include pinning her against the lockers and fucking the shit out of her. She strides past me after she's finished changing. I don't object to following her out because I have a fucking epic view of her plump ass. As we exit the gym she heads toward the side where her car waits. I reach out, grip her hand and drag her to my car. She doesn't fight or hurl questions at me. I unlock my car and she slips into the passenger seat like it's the most normal thing in the world.

Neither of us says a word as I peel out of the lot. My phone begins to ring immediately and I smirk when I see Gage's name flash. I answer the call through the cars Bluetooth.

"What?" I snap, and feel Koby's eyes on me but ignore her.

"What are you doing, brother?" I white knuckle the steering wheel, we may share blood but that doesn't mean shit.

"Whatever the fuck I want! Mind your business Gage—"

"You forget, she is *my* business." I grind my teeth.

"Not anymore!" I end the call not bothering to try tamper my rage. I love how it courses through my body, it makes me feel alive. I drive through the busy streets heading to the docks to meet King and Bishop. It was my idea to do this and I don't really give a fuck if she loses her shit and tries to fight. I'll make her fucking submit to me. I crave control—no, I need it. After everything that happened with Christine, I can't function without it. I thrive off the submission of others.

I slam the car in park outside the *Den*, it's out of the city where my brothers will never hear word of what happens here. In this place I'm not Knight Murdoch, I'm just a random guy who can be whoever he wants. I feel her gaze on me as I slip out of the car. By the time I round the front, she's already getting out and taking in her surroundings. I slide up next to her and wait for her to panic or try to run. The Den is dark and grungy, an old biker's pub that has been transformed.

"This the place where you're gonna try kill me, play-boy?" I smirk down at her.

"Nah, this is the place where you learn who I really am and that out of all my brothers I am the one you need to fear."

She doesn't look taken back by my declaration, all I see is intrigue in her eyes. Koby isn't like most girls, they would be screaming and clutching my arm in fear at being at a place like the Den. Biker's and fighters mill about but pay us no mind. The Den is neutral territory, so it doesn't matter who you are or where you came from when you're here. Everyone is equal. In a sense, I feel more like myself here than I do at home. No one judges you for your past or the fuck ups you have done. I grip her hand in mine and lead her toward the front. Kevin, the bouncer, spots me and pushes the door open. I ignore all the others that stand around and shout that they were waiting for hours.

I shoulder our way through the crowd, it's packed in here and you can barely hear anything over the roar of the crowd. I push my way through till we reach a small alcove near the back of the bar, pushing my hood back so Kenny the guard for the lockers can see me. He nods and steps aside allowing us through. I pull Koby after me and head to the back room where I know it will be empty. I release her hand and close the door after we enter, turn back and watch as her brow begins to crease. There is nothing in here except for two wooden chairs, a set of lockers and a bench seat.

"What is this place?" I ignore her question as I head for the locker and yank it open. I pull my hoodie and shirt off and shove it inside. I grab my tape and everything I will need for when Mav gets here, he's the only one who knows what I do here. "Knight?" I lift my gaze to hers as I answer.

"This is where I fight, you think the other night was a cash prize. That is chump change compared to what you can make here." Surprise flickers across her gaze as she takes me in. Before she can answer the door opens and Mav strolls in, he nods hello to her before coming to me and taping my hands.

"You good?" Mav asks as he straps my left hand. If I don't do this and go back with split knuckles my brother will ask too many questions.

"Yeah," I answer.

"Good, you fight then get the fuck out of here, got me?" I catch his stare, I see the unease in his gaze.

"Why?"

"Pauly's crew is out there. They may not be able to do shit in here but that won't stop them once you leave. I got Mike and Ronnie coming out to tail you home. Don't fight me on this." I glare at him, he may be here helping me but we aren't friends.

"Know your place—"

"My place is telling Bishop everything I know, don't forget that!" My upper lips pulls back in a snarl as I ready myself to tear him a new asshole, but Koby cuts in.

"I wouldn't make threats, considering you're the one betraying your boss right now. Imagine if Knight were to slip up and let his brother know that you knew he was here..." She whistles between her teeth and I have to fight the smile that wants to break free when Mav scowls over at her. Koby doesn't cower under the pressure of his gaze, she holds his stare with one of her own.

"Little girl, don't butt in and try and play with the big boys." It grates on my nerves the way he speaks to her, only I can fuck with her.

"Oh, is that all you got, big boy?" she taunts Mav.

"I'm not arguing with someone that should have been swallowed." Koby doesn't falter in her reply to Mav.

"Bitch, please, your birth certificate is an apology from the condom factory!" I can't hold it in, I throw my head back and laugh. I haven't laughed this hard in years. Mav is looking at me like he wants to put a knife in my chest as Koby's shoulder shake with silent laughter. He finishes strapping my hand, then storms from the room like a toddler.

Chapter Eight

Koby

I stand on the side of the ring and watch as Knight toys with his opponent. He taunts him, plays with him when anyone with eyes can see Knight is in control of this fight. The other guy is stupid to think he has a chance. His hits are all over the place and he never keeps his face guarded. He could have been knocked out in the first round but Knight is loving playing with him. The sight of him shirtless with sweat glistening off his chest... I had no idea he had a tattoo on his back. It's Mother Mary praying with rosary beads on her hand.

The other strikes out and manages to clip Knight across the jaw. I see it then, the carefree look in his brown eyes changes instantly. My eyes widen as I watch his eyes glass over, almost like he has zoned out and allowed someone else control of his body. He lands two blows to the kidneys before cocking his right arm and hitting right in the middle of his face. There is no way his nose isn't broken. The guy drops to the ground like a sack of shit as the crowd erupts screaming the *Viper* over and over again. Knight snaps his gaze to me. I lift my hands slowly and clap whilst cocking a single brow at him. I can see him fighting a smirk, he doesn't fuck around or gloat in the glory of his victory, he exits the makeshift ring and marches toward me.

He stops directly in front of me, ignoring everyone around us as they touch him and congratulate him on his win. The heat from his body soaks into me. I dart my tongue out to moisten my lips causing him to snap. He grips my hands and pulls me after him back toward the locker room we exited earlier. No sooner are we in the room, he kicks the door shut and pins against the wall, smashing his mouth to mine. I open for him without a fight. What's the point when he knows I want him. I snake my arms around his neck. He grips the backs of my thighs and lifts me without breaking our kiss. It isn't pleasant, our teeth clash as we fight for dominance. I grip the strands of his hair and pull—hard. He growls into my mouth before breaking the kiss and biting and sucking along my neck. I lock my legs around his waist when he grips my shirt and yanks it off, rips the cups of my bra down, then squeezes my nipples making me cry out. He bends down and captures it in his mouth sucking on my nipple hard. I grind against him and gasp when I feel how hard he is.

He switches sides and pays my other nipple the same amount of attention. I'm a panting mess and know I have soaked through my fucking thong. I'm woman enough to admit that Knight Murdoch has had my attention since the first time I met him back at my hotel. There is something truly dark and alluring about him that sucks me in and wants to bathe in the darkness inside him. He reaches back, untangles my legs, then slides me down his body until I land on my feet. He doesn't pause as he grips the waistband of my pants and yanks them down. He leaves my thong on, then gazes up at me with a lustful look in his eyes.

"Arms above your head and don't fucking move them." The rough sound of his voice sends shivers down my spine, making me do as he says. He lifts one of my legs and throws it over his shoulder. I watch transfixed as he leans forward and runs his nose along my sex inhaling. "Fuck, you smell so good." Slightly embarrassed by his comment I stand still and don't answer.

He reaches out and pulls my panties to the side. He doesn't fuck around, swiping his tongue through my folds and I cry out. He reaches up and twists my nipple between his fingers while his other grips my ass and pulls me forward. He pushes his tongue inside my pussy causing me to buck my hips, my body taking control and begins to ride his face.

"Oh fuck!" I moan when he sucks my clit into his mouth. I'm not the type of girl that can come fast. It takes me time and normally guys don't care enough to make sure a woman comes, as long as they do that's all they care about. Not Knight, the way he knows where to swipe his tongue and how much pressure is needed has me wanting to come already. "Knight... fuck, don't stop." I feel my orgasm building, it's right there within reach, I slam my eyes closed and prepare myself for it to hit.

"Nope." I snap my eyes open and glare down at him when he pulls back pushing my leg from his shoulder. I'm so fucking stunned, I don't know what to say. Seriously he's going to deny me that? Before I gather my thoughts or scream at him he pushes his pants down, his cock smacks against his stomach causing my own stomach to twist. There is no way a teenage boy should have that big of a cock!

It's long and thick. Fuck me, Knight is circumcised!

He steps into me, grips my face then slams his mouth against mine. I moan when I taste my own arousal on his tongue. He grips my ass then lifts me. I grip the tops of his shoulders and lock my legs around his waist. He pulls back and stares into my eyes.

"I slip my dick inside you, that means something, okay?" I furrow my brow slightly confused.

"What?"

"I don't just fuck anyone, Koby. I'm not like Rook. If I fuck you, that means something, okay." I search his gaze for a meaning but can't find one.

"I don't understand what you're asking me," I say honestly.

"It means, if you plan to fuck around or fuck me and my family over, say it now. I won't fuck someone who plans to fuck with my head... I can't do that again." I cup his cheek, his honesty softening me. I kiss him hoping he can feel it through my kiss that I don't want to hurt him. I'll try with everything I have to make sure my freedom doesn't hurt him. He pulls back and looks up at me waiting for an answer.

"I won't hurt you or your family, Knight." *Not intentionally*, but I don't say that part out loud.

"Good." He reaches down and lines his cock up with my entrance, slowly lowering me onto his dick. We both moan as he slowly disappears inside my pussy, inch by fucking inch! I'm so fucking wet for him that he slips inside me with ease, though there is still a slight sting. I've never been with anyone as big as him. I cry out when he slams the remainder of the way inside. He groans. I grip his face and kiss him as he begins to move inside me and fuck at this angle, I feel like he's in my fucking stomach.

"Fuck, baby, you feel so good," I moan as he slams inside me hard. I drop my head back against the wall.

"Your pussy is sucking the life out of my cock." God his dirty talk is fucking making me wetter.

"Fuck me, Knight. Make me come!" I beg. He smirks up at me as he slams into me at a brutal pace making me scream out with every thrust. I don't give a fuck who can hear me screaming, his cock is too fucking good! "Fuck, just like that. That's my fucking G-spot." He keeps his pace steady as he continues to fuck me, sweat dripping down the crease between my tits. I'm fucking done for when he leans forward and licks up the trail of my sweat. "Knight!" I scream his name as I come all over his cock. He doesn't pause or allow me time to come down from my high, fucking me harder, chasing his own release.

"Fuck... Koby," he cries out my name as he comes deep inside me. He flops forward resting his forehead against my shoulder. I drape my arms limply over his shoulders. The only sounds that can be heard is our heavy breathing, the roar of the crowd and the dim bass of the music.

Knight lifts his head and smirks up at me before placing a tender kiss against my lips and slowly pulling out of me. I flinch and he frowns in concern which causes me to chuckle lightly.

"Your cock is big and it just stings a bit." His chest rumbles as he laughs and places me on my feet. He darts his head side to side looking for something. "What's wrong?" I ask.

"I don't have anything to clean you up with." I suck in a sharp breath as I was not expecting that. I've never had a guy want to care for me after he came. I pat his chest and push him back a step as I pull my thong back into place.

"Let's get dressed and then find a bathroom so I can clean up." He eyes me for a beat before nodding. We dress in silence but it isn't uncomfortable.

Chapter Nine

Knight

I stand outside the bathroom door waiting for Koby, getting lost in my own thoughts. I haven't fucked anyone since Christine. The thought of fucking someone put me off because of what that bitch did to me. Don't get me wrong, Rook and I have shared plenty of girls but I've just never stuck my cock in any of them. Tonight, watching Koby at the side of the ring, and the way she looked at me when I came for her, made me so fucking hard that I couldn't think straight. I blurred the fucking lines tonight. I told her she couldn't fuck me over, when in truth, I'm the one who plans to fuck her over and ruin her just so I can have my freedom from my family.

When I feel a hand grip mine, I snap out of my

thoughts, peer down at her and smile. She is one person I don't know if I could ever share with my brother. Rook and I are identical so whenever a girl would want to fuck me, we would switch places and he'd do it for me. I shake my head to clear those thoughts as I lead us out of the Den. I feel them before I see them. I yank Koby in front of me and spin around to face them. Carlos and four others stand there with a wide grin on their faces. Koby slides up beside me, it pisses me off when their gazes turn to the blonde Russian at my side.

"You're not going to introduce us to your friend?" I sneer at AJ, he knows he can't do shit to me here. The fact that he hasn't taken his eyes off Koby has my blood boiling and my fist's clenching at my sides.

"He doesn't need to, you're not worth my time," Koby snarls as she grips my hand and pulls me after her.

"We'll see you real soon, baby Murdoch." I yank free of her hold and march right up to AJ until we are chest to chest. The men surrounding him move in, until he raises his hand, halting them. "You and your family are going down. We know your brother killed the Don of your family and he will pay for that." A dark chuckle slips past my lips as I stare at the under boss of the Polizzi family.

"I have no idea what you're talking about." He grits his teeth, I see it in his eyes and the way he tenses he was hoping I would snap and instigate a brawl so he would be cleared to kill me. That is the only way to get away with a fight here. You start it, then the other has the right to kill you. If not, the owner of the Den will kill you. "My family and I are still grieving the death of our beloved father. Tell Pauly we'll be seeing him *real* soon." I don't bother to wait for him to reply as I turn on my heel and leave.

"Where the fuck did this happen?" Bishop shouts from behind his desk. After getting home I tried to send Koby back to the guest house but she wouldn't fucking listen. She and I stand here in Bishop's office with him, Rook, King, Gage and Kiara. Mav and Luka walk in. Mav shoots me a look but I ignore it. "Answer me, Knight!"

"He took me to another fight," Koby answers for me, garnering everyone's attention.

"Oh, shit." I hear Kiara mumble.

"He did what now?" Bishop's tone is low. Whenever he gets quiet, that's when you know shit is about to get real fucking bad.

"I wanted to fight and Knight caught me trying to sneak away from Gage's gym." I can feel Gage's gaze on me but don't pay him any mind as I stare down at the girl beside me. Why the fuck is she taking the blame for me?

"Luka, Mav, show Koby to the bunker." Before Luka and Mav can move a step, I'm in front of her staring them down. They both pause as they stare at me.

"You so much as lay a finger on her, I'll fucking kill the both of you," I growl. They turn to Bishop, waiting for him to give them a direction on what to do next. Before he can answer, Kiara butts in.

"How about I take Koby back to the guest house to check on D and leave you all to talk?" She voiced it as a question, but we all know she's going to do it anyway. As soon as they are out of the room and the door closes, King gets right in my face. Rook takes Koby's place beside me ready to throw down for me if it comes to that.

"You stupid son of a bitch, now they know about her!" he screams in my face.

"So fucking what?" I yell back.

"They know now that we know about their deal with the fucking Russian's! We don't have the men to go against the fucking Bratva. If they tell her father she is here, we're all fucked!"

Rook shoves King back and stands in front of me. I love my twin but this isn't his fight, so push him aside ready to take whatever fallout comes next.

"I have just put King in charge of the Ramello family's territory." My eyes widen in surprise. "You will now take over the Ramano territory." Rage thrums through me, he has just chained me to this family and that wasn't the deal.

"I fucking told you I would get you the information from her for my freedom!" Rook spins on me, the hurt look in his eyes guts me deeper than the bullet that went through me.

"You want to leave?" I meet my twins gaze and hate that I'm hurting him. It's always been me and him against the others. I want to stay but I can't take the tension and the way King looks at me because of what I've done. I know I deserve it but it still fucking sucks.

"I have to, you know that." He shakes his head and slams his hands against my chest shoving me back a step.

"You fucking pussy-ass bitch! You are not fucking leaving. Do you hear me? We are a fucking family and I will not lose another fucking sibling because of this shit!" He spins back to face Bishop who is staring at me with a calculating look. "I'll take his place——"

I cut him off. "No, Rook."

"Shut up, traitor! I'll take his place. He can help us take down the other two families and then deal with Russians, but you know he can't lead. It's too much for him." I glare at the back of my twin's head—he swore he would never tell anyone.

"Why?" That one word from Bishop holds so much weight.

"Because he is still plagued by nightmares and flash-backs from what Christine did to him." Just like that, all the wind inside me rushes out and I drop into the chair cradling my face between my hands. My twin just sold me the fuck out.

Chapter Ten

Koby

Three days...

I haven't seen or heard from Knight for three days. I don't know what happened after I left him with his brother and the other two. I haven't gone back to the gym, hoping that I would be able to catch him at the house. No such luck yet.

"I want to go home." I turn toward Dimitri. We're sitting on the couch in the guest house watching a movie but I couldn't tell you what it's called as my mind has been focused elsewhere. I run my fingers through his hair and try to smile reassuringly. Dimitri is just a kid and wasn't meant for this life. I wish things had been different. I wish he could have had a better father. I wish we both could have had better parents, but life is fucked up like that. In order to save him from *that* life, I had no choice but to leave them behind.

"I know you do." He turns to look at me and the sorrow in his gaze guts me to my core.

"I miss them." My breath rushes out of me.

"I miss them too. We have to be strong and stay on course. We are holding up our end of the deal and soon enough we will be able to return home." The thought of leaving this place has a pang of sadness shooting through me. "How about we go for a swim?" He smiles wide and jumps up to race into his room and change. Dimitri loves to swim and I need the cardio of doing laps. I need to stay in shape to be ready. When the Murdoch's realize the truth I have been hiding, they are going to come for me. I just hope that Allison and Kiara protect Dimitri. I know Ally loves him and won't let anything happen to him. Me on the other hand, I know they will hurt me to get the answers they need to take down my family. The thing is, they think I'm her when I'm not. They think I'm the trump card but they are so very wrong.

We've been swimming most of the day and it warms my heart to hear Dimitri's laughter. Kiara, Ally and Mela joined us for a swim. Kiara, Mela and D are playing in the pool whilst Ally and I sit on the loungers watching them with smiles on our faces. It's hard to believe that I actually feel comfortable around these girls, given who they share a bed with. Their fiancés may be mafia lords but they don't parade around like most of the other wives I have encountered.

"What are you, Koby?" I turn to Allison, surprised to see her smile replaced by a look of accusation.

"What do you mean?"

"What are doing with Knight?" Her question startles me. I spy Kiara out of the corner of my eye swimming over to the ledge. The girl is fucking beautiful and has no idea. Her pale as fuck blue eyes and black hair make her any man's wet dream. "Koby?" I shake my head and focus back on Ally, she is just as beautiful as Kiara with her blue eyes and blonde hair. These guys sure know how to pick 'em.

"I'm not doing anything with Knight," I defend, not needing to explain to these two what Knight and I do. Her question actually pisses me off.

"Look." I turn to Kiara as she rests her arms on the edge of the pool and stares up at us. "Knight isn't like the others, he... went through some things."

"Some fucked-up things," Allison tacks on. They think I'm stupid, I know exactly what he went through. He may not have told me himself, but that doesn't mean I didn't do some digging and listened to conversations around me.

"What happens and doesn't happen between us is none of either of your business," I grit out.

"All I'm saying is, you fuck with him you won't just have Rook and the others coming for you. You'll have me as well. I love that boy more than you will ever know and I will not watch him be hurt again." The venom in Kiara's tone has me tensing. Her eyes have hardened and if she were anyone else, I would have punched her in the mouth for speaking to me that way.

"What Kiara means to say is." I spin around and it takes me a second to realize that it isn't Knight standing there, it's Rook. I still find it hard to tell them apart. The only reason I know it's Rook is because he isn't looking at me like he wants to equal parts kill me and fuck me at the same time. "Fuck my brother over and your Russian father won't be able to save you from what I'd do to you. My brother has been through enough. He is dealing with more shit then he can handle and doesn't need you fucking with his head." I've fucking had enough of this shit. I climb to my feet and storm past Rook. Just as I pass him, he strikes out and grips my wrist yanking me to a stop.

"Get your hand off her now!" I look to the back door and see Knight, standing there in a pair of black jeans and white plain tee that is molded to his body like a second skin. Rook doesn't listen to his brother. Knight prowls toward us like a panther hunting its prey and whacks Rook's hand away, before wrapping an arm around my waist and hauling me back against his chest.

"You're playing with fire, brother," Rook grinds out through clenched teeth.

"Lucky it will be me that gets burnt and not you," is all he says before leading me away from his family and Dimitri, taking me to the guest house. I don't say a word as he shoves the door open and marches us into my bedroom, before kicking the door closed behind us. He releases his hold on me and I put some space between us. I move to my dresser to grab a shirt so I'm not standing here in my two piece. "Don't."

That one word from him has me pausing and turning back to face him. I can see from his expression that he's distraught over something, I want to help him but I also can't get in too deep. Whatever this thing is between us won't last. Once they accomplish what they have set out to do, I'll be gone. I'll finally have my freedom for the first time in so many years, and I won't have to lie daily.

"What are you doing here, Knight? I really don't feel like getting another lecture from your family." His brows pull in.

"What did they say to you?" I release a loud exhale and hold his gaze. He has rings beneath his eyes from lack of sleep. His hair is a tousled mess. He's stiff and ridged which tells me something more is going on with him since I last saw him.

"They just told me not to fuck you over."

"That's what families do."

"Wouldn't know what that's like." I shrug my shoulders, his gaze softens slightly at my admission.

"Where is your family?" I tense up at his question. His eyes narrow, he knows I'm about to lie to him but I don't have a choice.

"Gone." It's the best explanation I can offer him. He closes the space between us, reaches out and I expect him to cup my face, but he doesn't. He holds my gaze as he reaches around me and pulls the strings of my top undone. I don't stop him as he reaches for the strings at the back of my neck and yanks them. My top drops to the floor but neither of us break eye contact.

"I know you're lying and right now I don't give a fuck. All I want to do is fuck you and forget about everything else." His whispered words have heat flooding me, I'm already wet for him. Just the sight of him arouses me.

"Okay."

"I can't be gentle, Koby, it's not in my make-up. Can you handle that?" A shiver rolls through me as I dart my tongue out to moisten my lips.

"Yes." No sooner is the word out of my mouth, he claim my lips in a searing kiss that steals my breath.

Chapter Eleven

Knight

Kissing her is becoming a habit I can't afford. The feeling of her soft plump lips as they move against mine has the stress slowly fleeing from my body. I need this, I need to get lost inside her to forget about the other shit. I never wanted to run things like King does, he's in his element running his territory alongside Bishop. I hate it. I fucking loathe it in fact. I'm strapped to a desk hacking shit. I have all the information I need and I should tell my brother but I... can't. Telling Bishop means giving her up and I'm not ready to do that just yet.

She fists my shirt in her hands, using it to pull me flush against her. I groan when I feel her nipples harden against me. I reach between us and twist them causing her to gasp in my mouth.

Reaching down, I pull the strings at the sides of her bottoms, and no sooner have they fallen away, do I reach between her thighs and cup her pussy. She moans into my mouth as I slide a finger through her slick folds. She is dripping fucking wet and I've barely touched her. I love how responsive she is to my touch. I grip the backs of her thighs and lift her. She locks her legs around my waist and runs her hands through my hair without breaking our kiss. I walk us toward her bed. I don't place her down gently, dropping forward, crushing her beneath me.

I grind into her causing her to moan into my mouth, I don't know what it is about this girl that has me going fucking mad. For years I thought something was wrong with me as I couldn't stomach the thought of a woman's touch. Every time I was touched by one, a rage so potent and feral would consume me to the point I would freeze up. I was transported back to the times Christine would hop on top of me and grind all over my dick until I got hard, then she'd fuck me. At that age I thought I was on cloud nine. Now, though I know I never loved her. In a way, she had raped me and made me believe that what we were doing was right and we were in love. How Allison and Amelia turned out so *normal* whilst sharing DNA with that crazy mutt I will never know.

Koby breaks the kiss cupping my face as she searches my eyes. I rest my weight on my elbows as I settle myself between her legs.

"Where'd you go just then?" I stare down at her in confusion.

"What?" She smiles lovingly at me and that throws me.

"You do that sometimes, you're here physically but I can see it in your eyes. Your mind wanders and... I was curious as to why you do that?"

I'm choosing to ignore that question, if I open up about where the fuck I drift off to she will never look at me the same. She can never know that the thought of sex transports me back to the times Christine used my body for her own pleasure. I kiss her to distract her from her line of questioning and within seconds she is moaning and writhing beneath me, grinding her pussy against me. She reaches between us and grips the bottom of my shirt, pulling up. I help her out and chuck it to the side before sitting back and shuffling out of my pants.

I love the way her eyes drink in my nakedness. Koby is the first woman to ever hold my attention and keep me out of my own head. It's almost like she is my own personal brand of heroin. I can't be slow, I need to get lost inside her and escape everything that is running through my mind. I line my cock up and slam inside her without warning, she cries out and I pull out almost all the way before slamming inside her again, the force shifting her body up the bed.

"Knight!" I love hearing her scream my name. I keep thrusting inside her hard, punishing her body. I can feel her cunt sucking the life out of my cock, she's close already. I lean and bite on the soft flesh on her neck sucking as I go so I can leave my mark. A thrill runs through me at the thought of everyone seeing my brand on her. I feel a draft but ignore it, I already know who it is that just came in the room. Koby gasps and pulls me flush against her to use my body as a shield. I stop fucking her and look over my shoulder at my twin who just casually leans against the wall staring at us.

"What the fuck?" Koby shouts. Rook darts his gaze between the two of us before finally settling on me. I know what he's thinking before he even voices it.

"I want to play." I feel Koby tense beneath me as I stare at my brother. I see the challenge in his eyes. If I deny him this, he will know Koby means more to me than I have led him to believe. I look back to Koby, her eyes are wide. I see the uncertainty in her gaze but the look of trust I see in them steals my breath. If she was anyone else, I'd tell Rook to fuck her while I shoved my cock down her throat to keep her quiet but, she isn't anyone else. She is the girl that has me by the fucking balls without even trying.

"Knight?" The sound of my name whispered from her sinful lips shakes me from my tormented thoughts. "I don't want your brother." Those five little words mean so much more to me then she will ever know—every girl wants the twin fantasy. They want both of us worshipping them and fucking them like there is no tomorrow. Not Koby, she could have the both of us right now, she doesn't want that though, all she wants is... me.

I look back to my twin. He's closed his emotions off from me but that doesn't stop me from being able to read him. I'm about to drive a wedge between us by declaring our enemy as my own.

"She's mine." Two words, two words I never thought I would ever utter in my life. Rook's face morphs into surprise at my declaration. He doesn't say another word as he leaves the room, closing the door behind him.

"Yours, huh?" I stare down at Koby and smile.

"Yeah, mine," I say before capturing her lips in a kiss of ownership. This thing between us is something I may not have wanted or ever seen coming but now that I have it, I don't think anything could make me let her go. I deepen the kiss as I thrust inside her again, making her legs wrap around my waist pulling me in deeper. I grind against her and relish in the gasp that escapes her. I may have just figured out that she means more to me than I wanted, but that doesn't mean I'm the type of guy that makes love to his woman. No, I like to fuck. I quicken my pace, slamming into her over and over again until she screams my name loud enough for everyone to hear as she comes all over my cock. I keep fucking her chasing my own release.

"Oh, God!" she moans as her body bows off the bed, aftershocks continuing to wrack through her tiny body. I pull out of her and rest back on my haunches as I pump my cock in my hand. Her eyes trail my every move. Her mouth parts slightly as she watches me pump my cock, her tongue darting out to moisten her lips as she waits. I throw my head back and roar out my release as jets of come spurt all over her stomach, tits and neck. My breaths are coming in short rapid pants as I stare down at the masterpiece I just painted all over her body. I reach down and smear my cum all over tits before pushing a single finger against her lips. She opens for me.

"Suck." She does as I ask and moans at the taste of my cum on her tongue. This girl has me hardening again just from that small moan.

"What the fuck are you doing, brother?" I turn away from the desk in the corner of my room and face Rook. I knew this conversation was coming, which is why I left Koby after fucking her again. I hate to admit but I didn't want to leave her. I've been waiting over an hour for Rook to come in and argue with me over my decision.

"It's none of your business," I grit out. He throws his hands in the air, marches over to the bed and sits on the edge.

"It is though. You know Bishop only let her stay here because he needs information about her father!" The reminder of who she is and where she comes from has me gritting my teeth. I've been tracking her every move, hacking every network I know of to find any information on Anya Volkov. The girl is like a fucking ghost, she doesn't exist. All I can find out so far is her age. She is twenty-one, so I know she has lied about her age. That doesn't bother me, she may be a couple years older than me but fuck it. "You've fucking fallen for her and you know she is going to end up in King's clutches even if you don't like it."

I fly out of my chair. Rook jumps to his feet with me in his face within seconds. My hands clench into fists at my sides. I've never fought with Rook, it's always been him and I against the world, but right now, I want to ring his fucking neck. Koby will never end up in King's torture chamber.

"He lays one fucking finger on her and he'll meet his maker before his daughter's sixth birthday." Rook shakes his head and pushes in closer until our foreheads touch.

"You stupid son of a bitch, she is a job, Knight! You were supposed to get information on her and report back to Bish, not fall in fucking love with the first girl who gets your cock wet." I don't think, rage blinds me as I strike out and punch him in the face. Shocked by my own actions, I stumble back a few steps and watch as he swipes the trickle of blood from the corner of his mouth.

I just hit my fucking brother!

Rook straightens and turns to me, the look in his eyes has me hating myself even more. The look of disbelief kills me. We've always been each other's protectors, until now. I turned on the one person who has always been in my corner because of Koby.

"Rook..." He raises his hand. I snap my mouth closed and wait for him to berate me and tell me how much of an asshole I am. He doesn't do any of that. Instead, he just shakes his head and walks out of my room, leaving me to wallow in my own self-hatred

Chapter Twelve

Koby

Sweat drips down my body. I keep my guard up as I move left to right under the elastic bands that Gage has set up across the ring. He has been pushing me hard and training me harder as I have a fight coming up in a week. I haven't fought since the night Knight showed up and I need the cash. I may stay with the Murdoch's but that doesn't mean I allow them to pay for anything. It was too risky allowing Anya to send us money, she would be the first-person Vlad would have gone to when we fled.

"Focus!" The sound of Gage's booming voice pulls me from my thoughts. I continue through my workout and retrace the same steps I have been doing for the past two hours. My body is aching, but I thrive off of it. Feeling the aches and pains always makes me feel more alive. I slouch against the ropes breathing hard as soon as I finish. I drop to the mat and rest back in the corner of the ring as Gage makes his way inside. He hands me my water bottle. I drain the bottle completely before accepting Gage's offered hand, he claps me on the shoulder once I'm on my feet.

"That was a fucking work out," I wheeze out. He chuckles.

"Good, you need to get in shape for this fight." I balk at the asshole.

"I am in good shape, thank you very much!"

"I agree." We both turn our heads to see Knight leaning against the back wall with his hood up, shrouded in the shadows. I nibble my bottom lip slightly, excited to see him here. The past few nights have been spent with him in my bed and between my legs. I need to end things with him before I become more attached than I already am, but it's fucking hard. I want to keep him, I want to see where things go with us but once he finds out the truth, he'll hand me over to his brother and I'm as good as dead.

"Go on, you've done enough for the day." I beam at Gage before jumping out of the ring and heading to the locker room to grab my things. I grab a shirt from my locker and throw it over my sports bra, then grab my phone and head out to meet Knight. I head toward the back where I saw Knight standing but he isn't there. I decide to head to the front, thinking he might be out sending my driver home. Instead, I find him inside his car. I head toward his car and slip into the passenger seat. I expect him to kiss me like he has been doing each time we see each other, but he doesn't. He doesn't even say a word as he peels out of the lot, keeping his hood up, shielding his face from me.

Something is off, I can feel it in the pit of my stomach. My instincts have never failed me so when he passes the turn that would lead back to the house, I know something is wrong. I shift in my seat and turn to face him. I study the side profile of his face and that's when it dawns on me.

"Where the fuck is Knight?" I snarl at his twin. A smile stretches across Rook's face as he pushes the hood from his head.

"What gave me away?" I huff out my annoyance before answering him.

"You seriously think I don't know what the guy I'm fucking looks like? Or that I can tell the difference between you and him?"

Rook laughs but it's hollow and has no humor to it. He grips the steering wheel in a death grip causing his knuckles to turn white.

"Yeah, well, my twin needs to wake the fuck up and realize you're the enemy." The hatred in his tone is clear. I don't give a fuck what he thinks about me. His opinion is irrelevant to me. I don't give a fuck about him!

"Turn the fucking car around now, Rook!" He takes the next corner so fast the back end of the car slips on the wet road. I grip the oh shit handle above my head and reach for my phone in the center console. Rook is quicker than me. He grabs my phone and tosses it out the fucking window! "What the fuck?" I scream at him.

"You are not calling my fucking brother. You are nothing more than a fucking distraction. His head isn't in the game because of you! He needs to focus right now and your lying ass is fucking with him!"

"I haven't done shit to your brother—"

"You lying bitch. We know Koby isn't your real fucking name!" I tense and clamp my mouth closed. Rook chuckles darkly. "See, you're all bark and no bite aren't ya, Anya?" My blood turns to ice at the mention of her name. They all think I'm her but they are so wrong. I keep my mouth closed as he continues to weave us through the darkened streets, the rain begins to pour making it hard to see out of the windshield. Rook doesn't ease off the gas. He continues speeding, making worry churn inside me as we leave the city limits and head toward the port.

"Why are you taking us to the docks?" I ask as I grip the door handle ready to launch out of the car as soon as he slows down. If he plans to kill me, he's going to have to fucking catch me because I won't go down without a fight, that's for fucking sure. He ignores me as he continues to drive. We keep driving through the horrendous rain until we reach the hill that overlooks the docks below. I grip the handle, ready to launch from the car but he clicks the locks in place before placing the car in park and turning to me.

It's too dark out to get a clear view of his facial expression. What I can feel though, is the hatred from his gaze pinning me in place. I remain still and wait for him to explain what the fuck is going on and why we are here.

"You have three minutes to explain before I drag you down there."

"Explain what and drag me where?" He grinds his teeth so hard I can hear it from my side of the car. He doesn't respond, just clicks the locks, exits the car and comes round to my side. He wrenches my door, immediately I kick out and throw a punch that connects with his jaw. He grunts and grabs my arms before I can scream, pushes me inside the car and covers my mouth with his hand, using his body weight to hold me still. His face is so close to mine, I can feel the heat of his ragged breaths fanning across my face. All the training with Gage is useless in this position.

"You are going to keep your fucking mouth shut! I'm taking you down there and you are going to watch and explain to me who each of these motherfuckers are!" I search his gaze trying to decipher what he means but I come up blank. "Nod if you understand."

I nod, he shoves off me and I drag in a ragged breath as I glare at him. The rain is pelting down on him but he seems unfazed by it, he flicks his head nodding for me to follow him and I do. We trek down the hillside, staying low and quiet. A shiver of unease rolls down my spine, something feels... off about this whole thing. My foot slips and I nearly slide down the steep bank but Rook reaches out and grips my arm halting my fall.

"What are we doing?" I whisper shout. He scowls at me before darting his gaze around, then points down to a cargo ship that is being unloaded.

"A shipment has just come in."

"And?" I growl, while still keeping my voice low.

"Your fucking daddy is still doing deals with Pauly and Vinny. Girls are being shipped here weekly and you're going to help me stop it." I reel back in shock. He has it all wrong, so fucking wrong. I don't get a chance to tell him that before he is dragging me after him. When we reach the dock, we stick to the shadows, staying hidden from the workers. We dart behind the buildings. When the building Allison and I were held in comes into view, my breath hitches as memories begin to resurface. The trauma my friend suffered at the hands of others will forever haunt me. We stop a building away from a group of men who stand in front of a container in the pouring rain. I squint my eyes trying to get a look at what is inside the metal box. I run my gaze over each of them cataloging their features and stances to memory—it's a skill that has been ingrained in me since I was a child. The man with the bulb shaped nose and receding hairline steps forward reaching inside the container. A scream pierces the air and my insides turn to ice when a young girl is yanked out by her hair.

The girl is dressed in what can only be described as rags. Her long blonde hair is a wet matted mess and I can see the fear in her eyes from here. My stomach churns at the sight of her, she can't be any fucking older than nine or ten. These sick fucks have brought her here to hook her on drugs and pimp her out on the nearest corner to make a buck off her body.

"This bitch is coming home with me first," bulb nose says, the others around him laugh like everything about this situation is okay. Rook's grip on me tightens, that's when I notice I have unconsciously taken a step forward. He shakes his head in warning. I glare at him.

"We have to do something!" I snarl. He slaps his hand over my mouth and shoves me against the building, keeping me pinned there by the weight of his body. I feel his lips brush the shell of my ear, a shiver doesn't roll through me like it does when it's his twin's lips are on me.

"Who the fuck is sending these shipments, *Anya?!*" I

shake my head, unable to answer his question because I don't know. "See, I think you're fucking lying and those girls are paying the price for lies." I fight against his hold, shoving him back a step before crowding him again.

"I don't know who the fuck they are!" His gaze searches mine for a minute before his eyes widen, a cool smirk touches his lips.

"You dirty little liar, I can see it in your eyes. You know exactly who they are and who sent these girls." I don't deny him, what's the point when he can see the truth in my eyes. Before he can question me on it more, a car pulls in and stops near the men. He slinks against the building hiding in the shadows as we watch. I brush my wet hair from my face, straining my hearing and trying to see as best I can through the rain. I watch as a man exits the car and within a minute of him and three others exiting the idling vehicle, everything turns to shit. Shouts erupt, more cars pull in and shots ring out. When the driver of the first car spins around I gasp, Rook's arm wraps around my waist as he tries to haul me back the way we came but I'm frozen.

"There she is!" he yells as he points in our direction.

Chapter Thirteen

Knight

I sit here and scroll through all the information I have on Koby and the Russian's. I find links between them and Pauly and Vinny. I don't see how the other families were able to gather the intel they would need to make contact and be able to fulfill these orders with Bratva if they didn't have an inside man! There are only a few that are trusted enough to be present when we discuss things, and my mind immediately swings to Gage. I may not trust the fucker but I also know he wouldn't betray Kiara or the other girls. He may not trust us, but he sure as fuck wouldn't hurt the girls. But if it's not him then who does that leave us with?

I growl as I rock back on my chair and scrub my hands down my face. I need a fucking break from this shit. I've been holed up in my room for hours trying to figure this shit out. I may get lost inside Koby every night but that doesn't mean she isn't the rat and I need to accept that. I've bugged her phone and make sure to check her calls and messages daily. The girl doesn't fucking talk to anyone outside of this house. I stand and exit my room, as I make my way to the kitchen to grab a beer, I round the corner and slam to a halt. Bishop, King, Kiara, Ally, Mela and Gage all stand around the kitchen island eating takeout. Their gazes swing my way but I'm focused on one person only.

"Where the fuck is she?" Bishop and King both swing their gazes to Gage, who looks just as shocked to see me as I am him.

"Dude, what the fuck are *you* doing here?"

"I fucking live here," I grit out through clenched teeth. I spy Ally out of the corner of my eye pick Mela up and take her from the room, she doesn't like us cussing around her daughter. Kiara hops off the counter top that she was just sitting on and steps between Bishop and Gage ready to defend her best friend if it comes to it.

"Then you should know where the fuck she is, dude!" Gage snaps. I stalk toward him but slam to a halt when Kiara darts in front of him. Bishop glares at me in warning. If I hurt his fiancée in the process of getting to Gage, he'll beat my ass for it.

"Someone want to share what the fuck is going on here?" King asks as he looks between me and Gage.

"Where the fuck is Koby you fuck-bag!" I shout. Gage's brows furrow and he looks genuinely confused for a moment before his eyes widen and he darts his gaze around the kitchen.

"Where the hell is Rook?" he asks.

"What does Rook have to do with this?" Bishop demands, but I ignore him as I focus on Gage and ask.

"Why?"

"If it wasn't you at the gym picking her up then that means your twin brother played both her and me." Now my eyes widen and dread pools in the pit of my stomach. Fuck, what have you done bother? I spin, preparing to go in search of my brother and Koby but King grips my arm, yanking me back. I smack his hand away, which only causes to piss him off. He gets right in my face. I don't back down, holding my ground as I meet his heated stare.

"You are not going off halfcocked. We'll go with you but you need to calm the fuck down!" I stare at him for a beat slightly shocked, after everything I have done to him, he still wants to...help me.

"Why?" A small smile tugs at his lips, placing a hand on my shoulder as he says,

"Because you're my brother, dumbass. Now let's go find your twin so I can beat his dumbass." I nod unable to speak past the growing lump in my throat.

"Wait, why did Rook take Koby? Can she not tell you both a part?" I peer at Kiara over King's shoulder, her question giving me pause. What if Koby isn't able to tell Rook and I apart? Is he trying to test her to see if she will fuck him? The thought of my twin burying his cock inside *my* girl has my blood boiling. Only I can fuck with Koby, no one else. If she turns out to be a spy, then I'll deal with it. The thought of hurting her has my stomach churning, I have no problem cutting any fucker but the thought of spilling her blood... makes me feel sick.

"I don't know if she would be able to, not how he was dressed." I step away from King and look to Gage.

"What does that mean?"

He shrugs his shoulders before answering. "He was dressed like *you*. Wore *your* clothes and kept the hood over his head the whole time. He stuck to the shadows and Evan even saw *your* car in the parking lot. He knew what he was doing and was actively trying to be you, Knight, but why?" I open my mouth to answer but clamp it shut. I actually have no fucking idea why my brother would do this.

"He wants information from her and thinks your mind is clouded because you're fucking her." My gaze swings to my oldest brother. I want to rebuke his claim. The knowing look in his eyes tells me I haven't been as discreet about fucking her as I thought.

"My mind isn't clouded," I defend as I hold Bishop's gaze. "I've been looking into her but I can't find the link between her and this fucking Vlad cunt."

"You can't keep her, Knight. She is the enemy." I grind my teeth so hard they begin to ache. Bishop may be the Don of this family but he can't fucking tell me who I can and can't fuck.

"Fuck you, Bishop. I know what I'm doing—"

"No, you fucking don't! You think your fucking slick but believe me, little brother, you aren't!"

"You don't know shit," I yell. Bishop raises a single brow as he runs his gaze over my face.

"You think I don't know you're the one that blocked Luka from hacking the Russian's server, or that you are the one who wiped all the records of Koby from my computer? I also know you are the one who rushed the adoption and birth certificate for King so he didn't have to jump through hoops to prove shit." I feel King's gaze boring into the side of my head but I don't say shit, what's the point. Bishop clearly knows I'm the one who has been pulling dirt and hiding shit from him.

"Why am I still alive then?" I say, barely above a whisper. Bishop being the bastard that he is, never breaks his poker face.

"Your blood of my blood, Knight. I would never kill you over something so trivial as this. In your own way I know you were only trying to help. Let me be clear on something though." I keep my gaze on him as he closes the space between us. "If that girl turns out to be a mole for them, I'll kill her before you even think to run with her." I hear the truth in his words. He would never allow Koby to live if she is a threat to my family and I wouldn't allow that either.

"Boss!" We all turn at the sound of Luka's panicked voice. He races through the front door, red faced and wide eyed. "We need to go now!" Bishop eliminates the space between him and Luka.

"What the fuck happened?" Bish growls.

"The docks, there was a shipment and everything went south. We watched them like you said but then—" He clamps his mouth closed when he spots me behind Bishop, his eyes widen. "Oh shit." That's it, I push past Bishop and grip Luka by his shirt slamming him against the wall and getting in his face.

"What the fuck do you know that we don't?" I feel the others crowd around but they don't intervene. Luka doesn't seem scared or even angry just... sad.

"You need to get to the docks, Knight. The Russian's

showed up out of nowhere... I thought he was you because Koby was there!" I drop my hold on him as my blood begins to freeze inside me. "The Russian's shot Rook."

The world around me stops, everything inside me dies, just like my twin did.

Chapter Fourteen

Koby

We take off running but they come from every direction. Rook curses beneath his breath as he pulls a gun from his waistband. I turn to him and hold my hand out. He scoffs, so I narrow my eyes at the smug fuck.

"I'm all you have for backup so you best be handing me one of those guns." He shakes the gun in his hand.

"I only have one." I bare my teeth at the dumbass.

"I know you have two, you always carry two and a knife in your boot, so hand me the spare!" His mouth opens slightly but no words come. When the sound of more gunfire sounds out, closer this time, he snaps out of it and hands me his backup. I check the mag first before flicking the safety off and following after him. The heavy rainfall doesn't help us as we aren't able to hear if anyone is coming up behind us. The visibility is growing worse as the weather picks up, the only way we are making it out of here is if we work together and at least try to trust each other. I am not fucking going back to them, so if I have to tell him some of the truth, I will. I spin around finding Rook's skeptical gaze already on me.

"I don't trust you." Good, we're on the same page then.

"You have no choice right now. You brought me here, not the other way round. I am not who you think I am, Rook. I'm not even related to Vladimir Volkov." He reels back clearly taken aback by my admission. "If we get out of here alive, I'll tell you who I really am." He searches my eyes for any trace of dishonesty before nodding slowly.

"We need to get back up the hill and to the car. I don't have my phone and no backup is coming so we need to leave now!" I nod as I turn and move toward the next building. Rook is close behind me. I keep the gun drawn in front of me. I hear shouts coming from our left and keep moving alongside the building, staying as close to it as I can. I stop at the edge and poke my head out to check both ways before darting across to the big building in the middle. We still have to make a run for it from this building to the next leaving us heavily exposed. I take a step forward ready to break for it, but Rook yanks me back. I gasp when he fires a shot near my face. My ear rings painfully as I spin around to watch a body fall to the wet ground.

"Stay behind me. They have our location now and we need to run for it!" I nod. He takes off and I follow after him. I spy a shadow to my right and slow my pace as I take aim and fire off a single shot. The fucker drops to the ground, his scream can be heard which causes me to cringe. I chase after Rook and slam against the side of the building. My nerves wrack my body as we stand here and watch cars zoom past us, they are blocking every exit point... trapping us. "Fuck!" I peer around him trying to find another way out of here, shit! The roads behind us will be blocked off in a moment, the buildings will be searched... that only leaves us with one possible exit point. I look to Rook and I see the uncertainty in his gaze, which tells me this is his first gun fight without his brothers backing him up. I shove the gun in my waistband and grip his face between my hands.

"Listen to me, I won't let you die, okay. If we get captured you sell me to them and go back to your family..." He shakes his head, earning a growl from me. "Focus on your hatred of me, Rook. Let that build inside you and shut everything else off. You need to make sure you make it out of here. If you don't, it will kill him." His eyes fill with pain, he knows what I say is true. Losing Rook will kill Knight. He already lives half in the dark and half in the light, losing his twin would shroud his world in darkness completely. "We are going to make a break for the water, it is the only option we have."

"We'll drown, the waves are too strong!"

"Listen to me!" He clamps his mouth closed. "It is the only way. We make a break for it and jump. Don't think, just do it. Do not come up for air until we are under the other dock or they will kill us." He remains silent for a moment, but nods quickly when shouts can be heard from the building over from us. "Ready?"

"Yeah, let's do this." I take the lead, pushing in front of him and scan each way. The lights from the cars help me to get a better look of where everyone is. The container with the girls is now further away, so I can't see what happened to the guys there and if the other two Don's made it out alive. I fucking hope they didn't. I reach back and grip Rook's hand in mine, then hold my breath as I watch three men dart into the building beside the large one we hide behind. As soon as they disappear inside, I run, dragging Rook with me. I hear shouts behind us, then gunfire ensues as we continue to run as fast as we can for the edge of the dock. This is the most reckless thing I have ever fucking done, I never come into a situation like this unprepared. I grunt when I feel something tear through my shoulder, I've just been shot but thanks to the adrenaline coursing through my body I don't feel it. I hear Rook groan beside me but don't look, we need to keep going. An Escalade comes barreling toward us, so I push my legs faster, expecting it to run us down but it doesn't. It shields us from the gunfire. I watch as Mav jumps out and shouts for us to keep going.

"Koby!" I freeze at the sound of his voice. Rook jerks to a stop beside me. Gunfire stops, shouts can no longer be heard, I drop my hold on Rook as I slowly turn to the left. I don't need to see his face clearly, I can tell from the silhouette of his body that he is here. I spot the men beside him lift their guns, four of them have red laser lights aimed at me. I'm ready to meet my maker as I close my eyes and picture his face. Shots are fired but I don't feel a thing, the sound of Mav's anguish cry has me snapping my eyes open, only to be met with the deepest brown eyes that I am so familiar with.

"Oh my God," I cry as I watch him drop to his knees in front of me. I reach out and cup his face as tears spring to my eyes. More cars fly toward us, but this time they are on our side. Shots are fired but it all becomes white noise to me as I stare into Rook's eyes. "Why the fuck did you save me, you fool!" A crooked smile stretches across his handsome face.

"Losing me would hurt him, but losing you would kill him. Love him like he needs to be loved." I brush my thumbs over his cheeks and wipe away the tears that fall from his eyes. I can see he is in pain. I can tell from how pale he is that he doesn't have long before he's gone. Knight won't recover from this loss, losing Rook is going to shred whatever tiny bit of humanity he has left. I open my mouth to tell him he's wrong but a loud boom sounds out then I'm sent flying. The last thing I remember is hitting the water before everything goes black.

Chapter Fifteen

Knight

I stumble back a step and smack into something... no someone. Arms wrap around my shoulders but I see nothing, I feel nothing. What Luka says can't be true, my brother isn't a fighter. He doesn't get involved in any of this shit! He hates this life and just wants to play pro ball, party and fuck his way through college.

"Let's go!" Bishops booming voice cuts through the haze of my grief. I follow after my brothers, Gage and Luka on autopilot. I know Kiara is screaming something at us, but I can't hear anything aside from my own heartbeat ringing in my ears. I slip into the back seat, next to Luka and Gage, and barely have the door closed before Bishop is peeling out the driveway with cars following behind us. I sit here silently replaying the last moments with my brother over and over in my head. The last thing I said and did to him was unforgiveable. I hit my baby brother over a fucking a bitch. I'll never be able to erase the look in his eyes from my memory for as long as I live.

"Why the fuck was he at the docks, Luka?" King shouts, I can hear the rage in his voice. His anger feeds the blood-thirsty beast inside me, the need for the blood of my enemies coating my hands has me focusing and paying attention to the conversation around me. "It's your fucking job to watch them!" King screams. I don't feel an ounce of remorse for Luka. If that dumb fucking cunt did what he was paid to fucking do, my brother wouldn't have been shot!

"I don't know. Mav was watching while I was..." He cuts his gaze to me before looking back at King. "Trying to gather intel."

"You mean you were trying to back door hack me because you can't get through my firewall?" Luka's eyes narrow, I can tell I've hit a nerve. He prides himself on being able to hack anything but what he doesn't know is I learnt most of what I know from watching him hack over the years. Computers have always fascinated me.

"You know?" he asks. I don't bother to answer. Bishop takes a corner too fast in the downpour causing the ass end of the car to drift sideways making us grip onto something or risk smacking into each other. He's been silent since we left the house and I know not being able to be there to protect our baby brother is killing him inside. Gage's phone lights up the inside of the car, he places it against his ear.

"Where the fuck is my brother, Mav?" He's silent as he listens for Mav's reply. I don't realize I'm holding my breath until he speaks again. "We're on our way, clear the area and make sure it's secured by the time we get there or I'm taking your fucking head." He doesn't wait for a reply as he ends the call, I never once thought about him and how he felt toward us. I can see it now and hear it in the way that he spoke. I may not view him the way he views us but Gage classifies us all as his family, and that earns some respect from me.

As the docks come into view my stomach bottoms out, there is a thick cloud of smoke, buildings are nothing but a pile of waste, some remain standing. How the fuck did this happen on our turf? Who would be so ballsy as to come into our territory and do this? Bishop continues to speed past the cargo that is set ablaze and the buildings that burn on our other side. It's like someone set off a bomb here. The car screeches to a halt and we all jump out. I pull my gun out ready to kill any motherfucker that isn't with us.

"Boss." I turn to where Luka is pointing. There by the edge of the dock, Mav and a few others are crowded around a... body. I don't think as I take off toward them, shoving the fuckers out of the way expecting to see my brother laying in Mav's arms but it's... Koby. Mav and her are both soaking wet. The rain continues to fall around us as I stare down at the girl I have been spending many a nights lost inside, unmoving and bleeding through her shirt.

"Where's Rook?" Bishop snaps, his voice has me snapping out of my shocked state. I bend down and grab her from Mav. He cuts a glance to me before releasing his hold on her, standing to his feet to meet his Don's murderous stare. Bishop grips the front of his jumper, yanking him toward him until they are nose to nose. "Where the fuck is he?" Bishop screams in his face. Mav shakes his head, Bishop releases him with a hard shove.

"They were going to kill her," Mav shouts, whilst blindly pointing toward the blonde beauty that is out cold in my arms. "He took the hit before I could get to him. Then the bombs went off and everything... it just happened, Bishop. I'm so fucking sorry."

Bishop growls pinning Mav with a look that promises fucking all kinds of pain. "Luka scan the fucking area and find my brother!" He turns to Dom next. "I want to know who the fuck was here and why, find me everything! No one leaves this fucking dock until my brother is found. Am I fucking clear?" A chorus of yes sirs ring out around us.

"How many times?" Gage's question is spoken so softly that it is barely heard over the rain, but there is no mistaking the rage underneath it. Mav doesn't pretend to act like he doesn't know Gage's question is directed at him.

"How many times what?"

"How many times was he shot? Where was he fucking shot? Was he able to survive the fucking shot or not?" Gage screams, it shocks the fuck out of me to hear the pain and anger in his voice.

"I counted four or five, in the back but I don't know whereabouts exactly he was hit. He protected her! I don't know what the fuck happened after the explosions went off. I saw her, I ended up in the water and found Koby. I sent the others to search for him."

"You should have fucking gone for him not her!" Bishop

yells over the pouring rain, I stand here and stare at each of them feeling nothing but rage. I want to fucking kill Mav and rip him apart until he begs for me to deliver the final blow, the blow that would never come because he needs to feel half the pain I feel right now.

"It wasn't just Pauly and Vinny, Bish. The fucking Russian's showed up, they're the ones that shot him."

The rain pelts down around us but I hear nothing except for Mav's words replaying over and over again in my head. I drop my gaze to the girl in my arms and stare at her, my fucking brother—my other half is dead because of her! I turn to Gage and shove her into his arms. He catches her before she can fall to the ground. I turn back to Mav, his gaze already on me. Whatever he sees in my eyes has him backing up a step, you're next you little bitch!

"Take her back, stich her fucking wound. Make sure she is alive and able to sustain what I'm about to dish out." Mav's eyes widen in surprise but it isn't him who answers me.

"Knight, I'll take care of her—" I pin King with a look that has him closing his mouth.

"He is my twin, not ours. I'll fucking deal with the bitch and I promise you this. She will fucking talk whether she likes it or not."

I feel my blood start to flow again, my body thrums with anticipation at the prospect of letting my most darkest part of myself out to play. Rook was the only in this fucked up world that kept me sane and grounded. Without him, I have nothing left to fucking lose.

Chapter Sixteen

Koby

Groaning in pain, I try to move but something keeps me still. I try to move my arms but can't. I slowly blink my eyes open expecting to find myself in my bed. My eyes widen when I look around the sterile white room. I look down and see I'm in a pair of sweats and a singlet, these clothes aren't my own.

Where the fuck am I?

I try to recall what the fuck happened and how I ended up here. Memories flash back through my mind. Tears cloud my vision the moment I reopen my eyes.

Rook.

I swallow the sob that wants to break free. I don't know what happened to him or if he is even alive! I blacked out after I hit the fucking water. Fear begins to rear its ugly head, I'm back where I started. They are going to kill me this time, there is no way I'm getting away from the Bratva a second time. I allowed myself to fall into a false sense of security by staying with the Murdoch's. I almost felt like I could be a normal fucking person for the first time in my life!

How stupid was I to ever think that I could be someone other than who I was born to be. I never lied to Allison, I really was born into the wrong family and my brother and I are the ones who will pay the price for that. I try to scan the area again to give myself something to do rather than get lost in my own head. My shoulder radiates with pain with any sudden movement. I turn to the side and I can see a patch of gauze that has blood staining it. Fuck, I was shot. My hands and legs are bound to the metal chair I'm sitting upon. There is a table in front of me that has a shit load of tools on it. Bile works its way up my throat, I know what they are used for and I need to prepare myself for the pain I am about to be in. I look to the right and see a hose curled on the ground, I run my gaze along the concrete floor and spot three drains, one either side of me and one just in front of me.

The sound of a lock turning has me tensing, I prepare myself to retreat inside my mind and ready my body for the pain that will be inflicted upon it. I saw firsthand what Allison went through and I know they will do the same thing to me. They are going to try and break me—mind, body and soul. I won't allow that, I need to make it out of here and get back to *him*. I don't know when or how, but Knight Murdoch became so much more to me than a casual fuck. He became the knight I needed to save me from the life I was born into.

The heavy metal door is pushed open, a man with a ball cap slung low over his face enters the room. Another follows, dressed exactly the same, all in black with a low-slung hat. Two more follow after, each of them stands in a corner of the room. I keep my mouth closed and watch for any sign of what they might be about to do. What I don't expect is for two more men to walk in, dragging an unconscious body with them. They drag the man to the corner and cuff him to the chains that hang against the wall. How did I not notice those before? Once the guy is secured the six of them walk out without saying a word or looking over in my direction. The fact they haven't said anything or even touched me makes me more uneasy than if they had just hit me.

I don't know how much time has passed before the man to my left begins to the stir. I'm exhausted, but the fluorescent lights above make it hard to fucking sleep when you can still see them through your lids. The man whips his head up and darts his gaze around the room. One of his eyes is swollen shut, the other is red rimmed and blood shot. His bottom lip is split, bruises cover his entire face. I may not be able to see any marks beneath his long pants and long sleeved shirt but from how stiff he is, I can tell his body would be black and blue beneath his clothes. When he finally notices me his eye widens ever so slightly before he masks his features. His upper lip pulls back in a snarl of disgust as he spits on the ground beside him.

"Predatel," (*Traitor*) he spits the word at me like I'm supposed to give a fuck what he thinks. The piece of shit turns his head to the side to show me the eight pointed star, the mark of the Bratva. I have no idea what the fuck he did to land himself in here with me. Frankly, I don't give a shit. I pull against the restraints and cringe when the burn in my shoulder intensifies, causing me to grind my teeth to keep from crying out in pain. "Ty umresh' za to, chto ty sdelal." (*You'll die for what you have done.*)

I smirk, making sure to keep all traces of emotion from my face. I'm not stupid enough to think this fucker isn't a plant to get me to talk. I also know there is no fucking way this room isn't wired with mics and cameras. If they think I will ever talk willingly, they have another thing coming.

"Prodolzhay govorit', suka, ya ub'yu tebya, prezhde chem vyberus' otsyuda." (*Keep talking bitch, I'll kill you before I get out of here.*) His eyes narrow as he breaks out into a rant, promising to cause me pain. I block out his bull-shit. He can make threats all he wants but the truth is, we are both just as fucked as each other. He may come from my motherland but that doesn't make us friends in any way. He made his choice when he decided to work for the Volkov Bratva, he signed his own death warrant.

Music blasts throughout the room making me cringe. It's so loud I can't hear a single thought in my own mind. I knew there would be cameras and listening devices but I never thought they would use *white torture* as a way to break us. Russian's use their hands and inflict pain on the body like they did to my friend over there. The bass of the song has my ears ringing, the screams of the lead singer has me grinding my teeth. The guy screams but I can't make out what he is saying over the music, it's so fucking loud that it grows painful as time ticks by.

I try to shrink inside my own mind but the bass of the same song playing over and over again won't allow me to hide. It's killing me that I'm unable to use my hands to cover my ears. I fight against my restraints hard, ignoring the pain in my shoulder until I feel the gunshot wound tear, then I do finally cry out in pain. I feel the blood soak through the gauze and slowly trickle down my chest, I slam my eyes shut and bite my lip to stop myself from screaming in frustration. He taught me better than this, he taught me how to ignore all the pain and breath through it.

Chapter Seventeen

Koby

My head lulls side to side from exhaustion. I've barely slept more than a few minutes. I don't know how much time has passed, all I know is I feel absolutely disgusted in myself because I've had no choice but to piss myself. It's the most degrading thing I have ever done in my life. Aside from the music that constantly plays on repeat that has my ears and head pounding, the smell in here is the next killer. The pig beside me has shit himself. I should thank my lucky stars that I have IBS and don't shit like normal people. The song loops again and I'm so close to tears because of it, I'd rather have the shit beaten out of me than suffer through this song any longer.

The ache in my shoulder burns every second of the day.

I know I have a fever and I fear I'm getting an infection from the wound not being treated or cleaned. If the Bratva's plan was to drive me insane and kill me from starvation, they are winning. My mouth is so dry I barely have any saliva left to keep my mouth moist. My stomach is constantly cramping from not eating for what I assume is days. That's not the worst part though, I need water so badly that it's all I can think about—dream about even.

"Eto ostanovleno" (*It's stopped.*) I startle at the sound of his voice. My ears are still ringing and his voice is barely audible over the ringing. A sigh of relief whooshes out of me at the silence in the room. I could cry tears of joy from not being able to hear anything. The sound of the lock turning has a burst of energy zapping through me. I'm sleep deprived and starved but the prospect of something new happening has me more alert than I have been in a long time. The door pushes open, six men walk in again all dressed the same as the last time. Four of them stand in each corner of the room whilst the remaining two stand at either end of the table that houses the tools.

I wait with bated breath for Vlad to walk through the door. The air whooshes from my lungs the moment he walks in. My jaw unhinges and my eyes widen in shock— what the hell is he doing here?

"You look surprised to see me, baby." His voice is firm but the anger that laces it gives me pause. His brown eyes burn unfiltered hate as he runs his gaze over me. He flicks his gaze to the guard that stands closest to him nodding toward the Russian that is chained beside me.

Oh my god!

They are *his* men. I'm not in Russia, I'm Knight's fucking prisoner!

"There it is!" My gaze flickers to him of its own accord, a cruel smile stretches across his face. "You finally realized you're not being held by your father." I feel the Russian's gaze on me as he is dragged to Knight and pushed to his knees. I fight the gag that wants to break free when I spot the trail of literal shit that followed him. Knight keeps his gaze on me as he asks my cellmate a question.

"You know her?"

"Da," the traitor answers. Knight's eyes darken with anger but I keep my face blank. He has drawn the wrong conclusion and I will not be the one to right it. How could he fucking do this to me? I mentally berate myself as soon as I think that. I have given him no reason to trust me, or even disclosed who I really am. I guess I asked for this in a way.

"Who is she?" he demands whilst still keeping his gaze trained on me. I brace myself for the pussy to rat me out and tell Knight exactly who I am, but he doesn't. Instead he throws his head back and laughs like a maniac.

"You fool, you have invited a snake into the lion's den and don't even know it." His Russian accent is thick. I didn't think it possible, but I am actually grateful to the punk for not snitching and trying to save his own ass. Knight grips the guy's hair and yanks his head back. Thanks to the cuffs, the guy can't even fight against him. Knight opens his free hand out to the side and within a few seconds one of the guards places a large hunting knife in his hand. Everyone in this room knows what is about to begin. I don't show weakness, keeping my gaze on Knight as he lifts the blade and begins to scalp the fucker. Two guards rush forward and keep the screaming Russian as still as they can while their leader goes about his business.

I thought the music was bad, don't get me wrong it was fucking horrific, but listening to the screams of this fucker is driving me insane. Blood is everywhere—splattered on the white walls, on the ground, some is even on me. Each time I've drifted to sleep, Knight has ordered one of the guards to slap me awake. After the third time, I mouthed off promising to kill the fucker. Knight stormed over to me and rammed his thumb in the bullet hold in my shoulder. I screamed so fucking loud, I couldn't stop the tears from falling. Being the sick fuck that he is, Knight smiled down at me and licked the tears from my face.

"What do you want done with... him?" The sound of one of the guard's voices pulls me from my haze. I snort drawing their attention. There is no *him* left, the guy is in fucking pieces, fingers, toes, hands, feet, scalp and even his fucking nipples are littered around the room. Every time he passed out from the pain, he would be given a shot of adrenaline to wake his ass up. Knight wanted him awake to feel every ounce of his rage.

"Clear it, every piece." None of them speak as they roll out a plastic sheet and place a blue tarp on top of it. The six of them begin placing pieces of the guy on the tarp. Once he is *all together*, they roll it up and duct tape it closed before carrying him out without backward glance. I slowly turn back to Knight when it is just him and me left, sweat coats every part of my body, my breaths are coming rapid pants,

I'm burning up. I know for a fact after Knight shoved his finger in my wound that I have an infection. I hope it kills me before he does. He lost his brother and he doesn't need to be the one to kill me. He already got fucked over once from the mother to his brother's daughter, he doesn't need to carry the burden of my death on top of that.

"Just do it," I rasp out, then begin to cough. His upper lip twitches as he runs his gaze over me. I must look like shit but I don't care.

"I wouldn't give you the satisfaction of ending things so easily. By the time I am done with you, not even your father will be able to recognize you."

It's not his words that cause me pain, it's the look in his eyes. He has retreated so far inside his own mind that I don't know if anyone will be able to bring him back. Which tells me one thing, Rook didn't make it.

"I'm sorry," I whisper.

"No, but you will be."

"I'm not sorry for what's about to come, I'm only sorry for your loss." That has him standing straight. His eyes hold my own without so much as blinking for the longest time. He moves so fast I don't even have time to tense before his hand is around my throat squeezing the life from me. I gasp for air, fighting against my restraints to no avail. The pain in my shoulder doesn't even register as the fight for my life ensues. Black spots dance in the corners of my eyes, my movements become jerky. I'm about to pass out. Before I can black out completely, he releases me with a hard shove. The chair doesn't move an inch, which tells me it's bolted to the floor. I splutter and cough, gasping for air. My throat is dry and coarse from no water. My whole fucking body aches and protests in pain.

"You don't ever get to mention him!" His angry voice reverberates around the room. I turn to the side and dry heave. I have nothing in my stomach to bring up, all that does is hurt my throat further. I take some deep breaths, gaining my composure as much as I can, before slowly turning back to face him. He stands a few feet away, vibrating with rage. His hands are clenched into fists at his sides. I search his eyes and can see how broken he is no matter how hard he tries to hide it. If he needs to hurt me in order to save himself from the darkness inside, then I'll take whatever he has to dish out because I care enough about him to allow that.

"Do whatever you need to do, I won't fight you, Knight."

"Who the fuck are you?" he shouts. I smile sadly at him and decide to give him a small amount of truth.

"I'm just a girl who was born into the wrong family, and never got to choose the path she wanted." He says nothing as he turns and leaves, locking the door behind him. I've never wished to be someone else more than I do in this moment.

Chapter Eighteen

Knight

I reach the top of the bunker and find Ronnie, Mike, Luka, King and Allison standing up here waiting for me. I ignore them as I turn to Mike.

"Get her something small to eat, enough to keep her alive and a bottle of water. Take two others with you when you deliver it. Unbind her but be ready, she'll attack you." He nods and heads off to do as I asked with Ronnie tailing after him. I look to the other three and cock a brow, waiting for them to say whatever it is that they came here to say.

"Bishop needs you to hack into the database and find intel on her brother." That is one thing I do respect about Luka, he doesn't fuck around or mince words. He gets straight to it. I know that must have been hard for him to say considering I am the one who blocked him. "One of these days, you're going to tell me how the fuck you used my own program against me, you little shit." I grin at the fucker and he shoulders past me toward the house.

"I can take over if this is too much." King's quietly spoken words have the grin falling from my face. I crowd my brother getting in his face, Ally pushes between the both of us shoving me back a step.

"He's only trying to help you!" I cut my gaze to her.

"I'll deal with her however I see fit. He is my fucking twin—"

"He was my brother as well, asshole!" King yells, causing Ally to flinch.

"Was?" King flinches.

"I meant *is*." I shake my head.

"Nah, you meant what you said. Don't fucking go near her, she's mine to fucking play with." I look back to Allison next. "If she doesn't break in three weeks, Bishop is putting an end to your blockade. I'm coming for the kid, Allison." Her eyes widen in horror. I don't wait for a reply as I turn and head back to the house to wash the fucking blood off me, then watch her on my laptop, torturing myself some more in the process.

***

One week later...

It's around two in the morning, I managed to get a few hours of sleep before nightmares plagued it. For the first time since I was a kid the nightmares don't involve Christine, they are based around Rook and Koby. I torment her every day and torture her mind, for nearly two weeks. I have kept her barely fed and watered—she's so sleep deprived, that I'm banking on her breaking within a few more days. I made a vow to her weeks ago that I would never lay a hand on her. I broke that vow when I choked her and reopened her wound. I've felt like shit ever since doing it, so I let Mike do the damage. The first day I let him punch her, I broke his nose the moment we left the bunker.

I hate that I can't allow myself to hurt her the way she deserves, she needs to suffer but I can't be the fucking one to do it! I can't even stand by and let the others do it. I tug on the strands of my hair as I sit up in bed. I reach over and grab my laptop, opening the lid, the video of her pops up immediately. The sight of her has me stiffening. I zoom in on her, what I see has me leaping from the bed and running from the house heading to the bunker. Ronnie sees me approaching and stands tall looking around for the threat.

"Give me the fucking key!" I yell. He digs through his pocket and tosses me the key. I race down the concrete steps ignoring the bite of cold on my bare feet, I'm shirtless and only in a pair of sweats. I shove the key in the lock then push the door open. I don't pause, knowing exactly where she is. I bend down beside her as she lays in a pool of her own vomit, a thick sheen of sweat coats her entire upper body. I roll her from her side to her back and rip the gauze off her shoulder and fight the gag that wants to break free. "Get the fucking doctor now!" I scream at Ronnie, who followed me in. I scoop her in my arms and race out of here, her body burning against mine. She is limp in my arms and doesn't even stir. I look down at her as I race across the lawn heading straight toward the house. Her wound is weeping with puss, the whole area red, inflamed and swollen.

I scream for Bishop and King as soon as I'm in the living room, place her on the couch gently and hear the thundering of footsteps coming down the stairs. I peer over my shoulder to see both my brothers in the same attire as me with their guns drawn. They lower their guns the moment they see me crouched beside Koby. They rush over and peer down at her, fear is clawing its way up my throat.

"What the fuck happened?" Bishop demands. Ally and Kiara come rushing down the stairs at that moment, both of them wear looks of concern.

"What's going on?" Ally asks. I shake my head, unable to answer their questions.

"Her wounds infected." The five of us turn toward the backdoor that I just came through to see Gage standing there with Luka beside him. I jump to my feet, flying across the room in seconds with him shoved up against the wall and my forearm pushed against his throat.

"How the fuck do you know that?" Gage doesn't falter in his response.

"Because I had Luka loop your feed so I could check her. She refused my help and antibiotics." His honest answer stuns me. I drop my hold on him and back up a step.

"Why?" Bishop's one word holds so much fucking power. If Gage answers him wrong he'll end up with a bullet between his eyes. He defied a direct order from the Don to stay the fuck out of the bunker.

"If you can't see what I do, then you're a fool." Sure enough I hear a gun cock behind me.

"Bish no!" Kiara pleads. Gage pulls his gaze from

Bishop to look at me, ignoring Bishop and Kiara as she tries to fight for his life.

"You can't harm her because you love her, losing... *him* hurts you but losing the first girl who has loved you for you would shatter you. I guarantee you, that is why Rook chose to save her instead of himself. He knew what she means to you, even if he hated it." His words have me stumbling back until I drop into one of the seats. Gage follows me and crouches down in front of me, placing a hand on my knee. "Loving her doesn't make you weak, Knight. Loving her proves you are strong, because being in this life, love will always cost you."

"Doc's here!" My gaze snaps toward the front door where Ronnie and the Doctor stand. Gage and I both stand at the same time moving toward Koby. The doc doesn't need directions, he spots Koby and moves straight toward her getting to work, he pulls things from his bag and lays them on the coffee table. He looks to Bishop as he pulls on a pair of latex gloves.

"Anything I should know?" Bishop cuts his gaze to me, the doctor looks to me expectantly. "I need an answer."

"I don't know what you're asking me." I say. He releases a frustrated sigh before he answers.

"Does she have any health concerns? Allergies? Chance of being pregnant?" His last question has me freezing in place.

Could she be pregnant?

"We don't know, can you just save the fucking girl, Doc. Her wound is infected. Treat that and we'll worry about the other shit later." I never thought I would ever be grateful for Gage, but right now I am.

Chapter Nineteen

Knight

The doc had no choice but to call in the help of his private nurses, two of them came to assist the doc. They cleaned Koby and her wounds, each of them shooting me disapproving looks, but I ignore them. They aren't fucking paid to judge or have an opinion. They're paid to fix us and keep their fucking mouths shut. The doctor set her up with an IV to get fluids through and also a bag of antibiotics. Bishop had Koby moved to the spare room downstairs. They have been working on her for nearly two hours and it's fucking grinding every nerve inside me to not know what's happening inside that room since the doc had King and Bishop drag me out.

"Knight?" The sound of Ally's voice breaks through my

inner thoughts pulling back to the present. I look around the living room to find Gage sitting in the other single chair. Kiara is asleep in Bishop's lap whilst Ally sits next to King on the love seat.

"Yeah?" My voice is coarse and rough.

"She's gonna be okay." How the fuck can she know that?

"Yeah," I spit out, annoyed. King pins me with a look that tells me I'm treading on thin ice talking to her like that.

"Why not ask the brother?" Bishop, King, Ally and I all turn toward Gage.

"What for?" King asks.

"He would be the one to know if she has any medical conditions." I grind my teeth hating that he might be right. I climb to my feet slowly, Ally follows my lead and blocks my path to the stairs that will lead me to Dimitri.

"Knight, please, he's just a kid!" Her plea falls on deaf ears. I gently move her to the side where King grips her around the waist holding her in place. I make my way up the stairs with her shouts following. I pause outside Mela's room door—Ally put Dimitri in Mela's room while she sleeps with them each night. I turn around when I hear footsteps behind me, then glare at Bishop and Gage.

"I don't fucking need you to help me!" I grit out.

"Too fucking bad. Now are we going in, or are we gonna stand and play with each other's cocks?" I scowl at Bishop but open the door none the less. I pause in the entryway, Bishop and Gage both at my back. Dimitri isn't asleep like expected, instead he sits on the edge of Mela's bed staring directly at me. For the first time since meeting this kid I see something more than fear in his eyes, resignation. I move toward him and he slowly climbs to his feet with his hands clasped in front of him. I leave a foot of space of between him and I, running my gaze over him and immediately know I can't hurt this fucking kid!

"I-is she dead?" I shake my head, his shoulders visibly relax.

"She's hurt." Dimitri swings his gaze to Bishop. "We need to know if she is allergic to anything?"

"N-no, she has IBS and that's it." I screw up my face in confusion. "Irritable bowel syndrome." I nod my head acting like I know what the fuck that is, but I really don't. "Is she okay?" He looks to me as he asks that question. I debate if I should answer him or not, but when his eyes begin to cloud with tears, I curse beneath my breath and answer the kid.

"The doctor is with her now," is all is say. Just because I won't hurt him doesn't mean I trust the fucker.

Dimitri and I lean against the wall outside the closed door of Koby's room waiting for the doc to come out. I keep playing Gage's words over and over in my head, did my brother really save her because of me? I've had days to ask her this question but the truth is, I've been avoiding anything to do with Rook. We refuse to hold a wake for him because none of us want to believe he is actually gone. The opening door pulls me from my thoughts. I push off the wall and stand straight watching as the two nurses head out, the doc is the last to leave the room closing the door behind himself.

"Is she okay?" Dimitri rushes to ask. The doc smiles kindly at the kid before focusing on me.

"I've cleaned and treated the wound, she has intravenous fluids and antibiotics as well. I've also put a feeding tube in..." I cringe internally, she has only been fed two or three times since I locked her up. "She has a couple broken ribs, a UTI from soaking in her own... mess."

"And the other thing?" I find myself asking.

"I've taken some blood. I'll have it rushed to the lab and we should have results within a day or two." I nod unsure what else I'm supposed to say.

"Can I see her?" I cut a glare at the kid. Doc places a hand on his shoulder, in a fatherly way.

"She needs to rest and recover. It's best for her to rest right now. It may take a couple days for the fever to break and for her to wake up." Dimitri deflates but nods. I thank Doc as he leaves. Dimitri turns to follow him, but I grip his arm and pull him with me. He doesn't struggle against my hold when he realizes I don't give a fuck what Doc says, I'm going to see her.

I stand frozen at the door. Dimitri breaks free of my hold and moves to her bedside. I can't stand the sight of her looking deathly. Turning, I storm out of the house. I don't think as I take off out the door and drop down onto the stairs out front, letting the early morning breeze cool my heated body. What the fuck have I done? Am I that fucked up in the head that I would potentially hurt the woman who could be carrying my kid?

"Fuck!" I shout as I stab a hand through my hair, angry as fuck. I never fucking wanted kids, they weren't part of my life's plan. I'm not cut out to be a... to be a fucking parent! I sigh when I hear the front door close. Bishop, King and Gage drop down beside me a moment later. None of them speak a word for a long time, each of us lost in our thoughts.

"What are you gonna do?" King's question has the air rushing out of me. If I had the answer to that I wouldn't be sitting out here.

"I don't know," I answer honestly. Bishop sighs beside me. I peer at him out of the corner of my eye.

"I know you... care about her but I need the information at whatever cost." As much as I hate myself for it, I nod my understanding. I don't hold it against him. He is the head of the family and has a job to do. Koby is the enemy and has intel we need in order to move against her family.

"I'll do it." The three of us turn toward Gage who sits on Bishop's other side. B scoffs, causing Gage to narrow his eyes. "Don't think I can break the girl?"

"How am I supposed to believe that, when you just admitted not long ago of trying to help her?" A sly smirk crosses Gage's face, an uneasy feeling spreads through me at that look.

"The easiest way to break someone is to gain their trust first, give me three days and I'll have the intel you need."

Chapter Twenty

Koby

I slowly blink my eyes open, immediately a soft moan tumbles from my parched throat. Something moves beside me and I recoil on instinct. The room is dark and the only light source comes from the small lamp in the corner. I should feel relief when I realize it's Knight who stands beside me with a cup with a straw in it, but I don't. I sink further into the pillow behind my head and look away. I'm in a room that I have never seen before. I lift my hand and cringe when I see a cannula in it. I follow the tubes that lead to IV bags hung on a pole beside me. I move my legs surprised that they are not bound as well, then shift my left shoulder and hiss. Knight crowds me once more but I pin him with a look that has him glaring at me in warning.

"Drink the fucking water. It will help." Begrudgingly I do as he says when he guides the straw to my mouth. I take a long drink. When I don't choke or cough, I keep drinking until there is nothing left. Knight places the cup on the bed side table before sitting on the edge of the bed. I grit my teeth to keep from lashing out at him. I know I said I would take whatever he dished out but I didn't think he actually would, then he got one of his lackeys to punch me in the face. The hit hurt, but what hurt worse was the fact he stood there and watched, not lifting a fucking finger to help me. "You need to tell me." His voice is barely above a whisper.

"I don't owe you shit," I croak. I've never expected anyone in this world to protect me or even help me for that matter, but the smallest fucking part of me hoped that Knight would be the first person in the world to do that for me. The fact he can't even look at me has me shaking my head and wincing in pain. I don't know what the fuck happened or how I ended up in here, all I remember is feeling dizzy and burning up then everything went black.

"I need answers, Koby, I need you to give them to me willingly or..." He lets his sentence trail off allowing me to draw my own conclusion. I snort, drawing his gaze back to me. His eyes hold pain and regret which just fuels the anger building inside me.

"Or what? You gonna lock me up and starve me again? Have one of your boys smack me around a bit?" He flinches in shame but I don't stop. "I never fucking betrayed you—"

"Then why the fuck did you take my brother to the ducks?" he shouts while climbing to his feet and pacing the room. I push myself up and groan in pain. Knight is at my side within a second. I smack his hands away not wanting him to help me in anyway. "Just fucking let me help you, goddammit!" I only relent because I'm in fucking pain. My right side is aching and I don't understand why, I never fucking felt the pain before now.

He helps me lean against the headboard but something snags in my nose. Reaching up, I feel a tube and try to pull it out. Knight smacks my hand away.

"Leave it in."

"What the fuck is it in there for?" He flicks his gaze away from mine as he answers.

"It's a feeding tube. It was the only way we could get food in you while you were out." My left arm twitches in anger but I tamper it down in order to ask.

"How long was I out?" He pushes away from me and paces the room, ignoring my question. "How fucking long was I out, Knight?" I shout at him.

"Six fucking days." That has my eyes widening, how the fuck could I have been out for that long?

Fuck!

"Where is Dimitri?"

"Upstairs sleeping, I sent him to bed a few hours ago."

"You sent him to bed?" Since when did Knight give a fuck about him? He runs a hand through his hair in agitation.

"I didn't fucking touch him, I wanted to but..."

"You lay one fucking finger on him——" That has him rushing me and getting right in my face.

"You'll fucking what? You forget where the fuck you are and who you fucking belong to!" I use my right hand, the one without the IV in it to shove him back but he doesn't even budge.

"I don't belong to any fucking body." I reach over ready to rip the IV from my hand in order to go in search of D and make sure he is okay, but Knight pins my arms to the bed. I thrash in his hold, ignoring the pain that radiates through my body as I try to break free.

"Just fucking stop!"

"Why?"

"Because I fucking said." We're screaming at each other. The door bangs open, causing us both to freeze. Bishop stands in the open doorway with his gun in his hand. He opens his mouth but a grunt is all that comes out when Allison shoulders her way past him earning a glare from the Don. She rushes to the side of the queen bed that is vacant and carefully climbs up next to me. Bishop flicks the room light on and I close my eyes to give myself a moment to adjust to the lighting. I blink my eyes open slowly but when I do it's not just the four of us any more, King, Kiara and Gage are now in here. I cringe, hating being the center of attention with all their curious gazes on me.

"How are you feeling?" Ally's question pulls my focus back to her. I muster a smile for her sake, not mine.

"Like shit." She cringes but I don't have the energy to placate her or ease her worries. Honestly, I'm fucking mad that she knew where I was and didn't do a fucking thing to help me. "Is Dimitri okay?" She smiles warmly at the mention of D.

"He's been okay but worried about you of course." Kiara moves forward and places her hand on my leg.

"I'm glad you're awake." I can't take this shit anymore.

"Why the fuck are you all here?" Both the girls eyes widen, Knight crosses his arms over his chest but doesn't pull his angry glare from me. The other three just stand in the back staring at me like I'm a circus act.

"We're here because we care," Allison says but even I can hear the goddam hesitation in her voice.

"You care?" I don't give her a chance to answer before I continue. "You're a fucking liar. I saved you and you fucking repay me by turning your back on me! Fuck you Alison, fuck you all." I reach over and tear the cannula from the top of my hand. Knight tries to stop me but he's too late, the feeding tube is next to go. I shove him back when he tries to stop me from climbing off the bed.

"Fucking stop or you'll hurt yourself!" he yells whilst trying to subdue me. Fuck him, I fight harder ignoring the pain. I manage to wrench my arm free and land a solid hit to the side of his jaw that has him cursing and letting me go. I push off the bed but the moment I stand, my legs give out. Knight catches me around the waist and a scream tears out of me the moment he hauls me against his chest. My ribs burn. "Fuck. I'm sorry." I freeze in his hold, did he just apologize? "Koby... please." I grit my teeth through the pain as I tilt my head to look up at him. The look he gives me is one I have never seen before.

"Uh, we're gonna leave you both to talk." Allison's words tell me I'm missing something. I hear them begin to move but my question has them all halting.

"Is Dimitri dead?" Allison whirls around to face with wide eyes.

"What, no, of course not."

"Then why the fuck are you all being nice, Allison." I struggle in Knight's hold but he won't release me.

"You both should talk," she hedges.

"Fucking tell me!" I scream.

"Leave!" That one word from Knight has his family nodding and exiting the room. Once the door is closed, he allows me the space I've been fighting for. I drop down on the edge of the bed and stare at him as he makes his way over to the window, keeping his back to me. My body radiates with pain but that I can deal with, it's the not knowing that is killing me.

Chapter Twenty-One

Knight

I stare out the window trying to gather my thoughts and figure out a way to tell her the truth. How do I tell her when I haven't even accepted the truth myself?

"You held me captive for fuck knows how long and yet you stand there with your back to me like a coward." Her tone is laced with anger and unease. She has every right to be pissed. I allowed my inner demons to control me and was led by blind rage. What she will never understand is that Rook is the one who grounds me. He is the one who keeps me from retreating inside the shadows of my past. Thing is, I only just realized that the demons of my past stopped haunting me each night I slept beside her.

"Hate me all you want, but I did what I had to in order to protect my family."

"I was never a threat to them." The conviction in her voice has me spinning around slowly to face her. Her face is etched in pain, but she isn't the type of woman to allow a bit of pain to hold her down.

"Not intentionally, but you being here has put them at risk." She opens her mouth but I push on needing to get this out. "I want to know what happened to my brother. Why the fuck were you at the docks?" She flicks her gaze away from me. I growl as I move toward her, grip her chin and pull her eyes back to me. "Keep your eyes on me. I want to see the truth in your gaze as you speak. Lie to me, Koby, it will be the last thing you do. I won't let my... feelings for you cloud my judgment any longer." She smacks my hand away and climbs to her feet. She sways slightly and I reach out and grip her hips to steady her.

"If you had any feelings for me at all, you would never have tied me to a fucking chair and left me to die." I keep my face blank, even though inside I hate I did that to her.

"Answer my question."

"Rook was the one who took *me* to the docks." I nod my head encouraging her to continue. "He came to the gym dressed like you. From a distance I couldn't tell it was him until we were in *your* car."

What the fuck was he doing?

"Did he say why he was doing it?" For the first time since she woke up her eyes don't shine with mistrust and hate, she looks at me with... pity.

"He wanted to prove to you that I'm the enemy."

"Why the docks though?"

"He said he knew there was a shipment, he wanted me to see it."

"How did he end up…" I can't even say it.

"There was a shipping container filled with girls. There were men there. He said their names were Pauly and Vinny. Shit went sideways when other cars pulled in, the guys were Russian." My hold on her tightens. I already knew about the Russian's being there from Mav, but the fact she is offering up that bit of information freely, has me second guessing my original thoughts. "They started arguing and then gunshots went off. Rook and I tried to flee. We got pinned down for a bit, so the only escape route was jumping from the wharf into the water."

"It was storming that night, the current would have dragged you both out." She nods.

"I was banking on that fact." I peer down at her and for the first time since I meet her months ago. I see it in her eyes, Koby is calculating and smart as fuck. "We made it halfway. I got shot and I think Rook did too but then a car came and shielded us. Mav told us to run but then…"

"Then what? What happened to my brother… I need to know… please."

"Vlad's brother was there, he called out to me and I froze. They had their guns trained on me ready to shoot." It shocks me when I see her eyes fill with… tears. "At the last second Rook jumped in front of me." I grind my teeth to stop the roar of anguish from tearing out of me. Her eyes take on a vacant look as she recites my brothers last words. "'*Losing me would hurt him but losing you would kill him. Love him like he needs to be loved.*' That was the last thing he said before I was blown away. I don't remember anything after hitting the water."

"We move on Pauly when the next fight is set. Knight will be the distraction for AJ while we move in." I nod as I sip my coffee. Bishop, King, Gage, Luka and I all stand around the counter in the kitchen. Ally, Mela, Kiara and Dimitri are sitting at the table eating breakfast. "You don't engage with AJ. You keep him distracted by fighting in the ring and that's it."

"I know what I'm doing, Bishop. This isn't my first fucking go at this shit." Bish pins me with a look, warning me to simmer down or he'll put me in my place. Growing up with older brothers always meant if we couldn't resolve shit with words, we used our fists more times than not.

"It's settled then. I'll take Knight to the fight, you, King and the others move in on Pauly which means we only have Vinny left." Gage seems to be here more often than not. He is actively taking part in everything to do with the family. He's earning Bishop and King's trust on his own without using the bond he has with the girls. I know having him around is hard for Bish since he slept with Kiara, but anyone with eyes can see Kiara is madly in love with Bishop and only views Gage as a... brother. He may have feelings for her but over time he has mastered the art of hiding it well from *our* brother.

"Once they are gone, then we make our move against the Russian cunts." I nod my head in agreement. I want those fuckers blood coating my hands for what they did to my brother. King sounds just as hungry for their blood as I am.

"We need to find a way in undetected. We'll draw too much attention if we all fly in." Bishop is right. Luka can't come with us thanks to his warrant, but it's not like the rest of us aren't noticeable either.

"We need an inside man," I say. We all exchange a look. Each of them knows I'm right, the problem is my brothers and I can't be the one to do it.

"I'll do it." My face scrunches as I look over Gage. "I'm the only one out of the four of us that could pass for a Russian." He isn't wrong, with his blond hair and green eyes he could blend in where we can't.

"How do you suggest to do that?" King asks.

"I'll figure it out. Someone in their organization must be able to be bought and get me in." Luka shakes his head cutting Gage off.

"The Bratva is a birthright, not some gang you can just join. You need someone with a higher standing to get you in and I don't know about you, but none of us know any Captain's."

"You don't, but I might." We all turn toward the entryway to see a pale looking Koby leaning against the wall for support. I want to rush and help her but I can't. She needs to do this and prove to my family she isn't the enemy.

"And why would we trust you?" Bishop's tone is wary and filled with accusation. Koby cuts her gaze to me as she answers.

"Because I'm offering you the head of the snake that took the life of your brother."

Chapter Twenty-Two

Koby

Knight searches my eyes for any sign of lies, he won't find any. I'm ready to help them take down the family that cost me everything. The Volkov Bratva took everything from me. Now it's my turn to take from them and finally be free of this life. I won't live like this anymore. I'm a trained weapon. I can read people, find information on them, shoot, kill, fight, - you name it, I can do it. That is how I was raised and what I was taught to become. I never got to play with dolls, I got to play with guns instead.

Bishop motions me to have a seat at the table with the others. It's then that I notice Dimitri. He charges toward me the moment I shoot him a smile and wince in pain when he wraps his arms around me. In the blink of an eye he's hugging me, then he's not. Knight has him by the back of his shirt glaring down at him.

"Don't hurt him!" I plead. Knight keeps his glare on D as he speaks to me.

"He hurt you."

"He didn't mean to, he's just a kid." It surprises the hell out of me when Dimitri looks up at Knight and I don't see fear in his eyes. He isn't even shaking like he normally would. Knight ignores my plea as he speaks to my kid brother.

"I told you to take it easy on her." Dimitri deflates slightly and it pisses me off. I keep my mouth closed because he seems... different. He isn't clinging to me or Allison for once, he actually seems comfortable with Knight. What the hell changed in the time I was away from him?

"It was an accident." Knight grunts as he releases D, then ruffles his hair playfully. Too stunned to process what the hell just happened, I let Knight lead me by my elbow to the table. I claim the seat between him and Allison. I don't even spare her a glance—I shouldn't have allowed her to get close enough to me so she would have power to hurt me. I did though and now her betrayal stings like a bitch. Bishop clears his throat drawing my attention to the head of the table. King sits to his left and Kiara to his right. I look around the table and notice Luka is present but Mav isn't.

"You have one final chance to convince me you aren't a threat to my family. If I deem you are, you won't leave this room breathing." The threat is clear. Truth be told, he isn't the one I'm worried about believing me, Knight is so distrustful that proving to him I'm not the bad guy is going to be the hardest task. "Koby?" I meet his stare. Bishop's face is void of all emotion. "Make me believe you because I don't want to hurt my brother by having to kill you." I nod my understanding. I flick my gaze to Dimitri who seems unsure and slightly terrified at what I'm about to do. I need to put his mind at ease.

"Everything is going to be okay, I swear. I won't let anything bad happen to you." He shakes his head and mutters under his breath.

"It's not me I'm worried about." I decide to unpack the meaning behind his words later. I take a deep breath before turning to face Knight, his gaze is already on me.

"I'm not Anya." His mask doesn't shift, his emotions remain walled off from me.

"Who. Are. You?" I inhale a deep breath wincing slightly from the pain in my ribs, once I tell him the truth, I will never be able to hide again. This persona I have built will crumble, never being able to be revived again.

"My name... my real name is Katarina... Antonov." The moment my last name slips from my lips Knight's eyes widen. I hear gasps coming from my other side but I don't look away from Knight. Silence ensues, no one speaks for a long moment.

"The Antonov Bratva was wiped out years ago." Now he's starting to get it. I nod, waiting for Knight to ask me what he really wants to know. "I thought you were Vlad's daughter."

I shake my head. Learning my name is one thing, but finding out who I am to Vladimir Volkov is another. Knight will never look at me the same after I tell him who I am to the Pakhan of the Bratva that now runs all of Russia.

"I'm not his daughter," I answer. Bishop's question pulls my attention toward him.

"Then who the fuck is Anya?"

"Anya is Vlad's daughter and my... best friend." Bishop looks to King. They exchange a loaded look before they both focus only on me.

"Why does everyone think you are her if you aren't even related?" King's question doesn't surprise me, I knew one of them would ask.

"Anya and I were both sent here to go to school, that is why I don't have an accent. We were taught by American nannies until we were twelve years old and sent here to the states. We attended St Mary's boarding school in Baltimore until we were called home when we were seventeen. I'm twenty-one, not nineteen." That piece of information doesn't shock them which alerts me to the fact they have been digging into my past. They won't find what they really want to know, as far as anyone in the world except the Volkov Bratva are aware, Dimitri and I died along with our family.

"Your family were all executed. How is it that you and the only male heir to your family survived?" There it is, the million-dollar question that is going to ruin everything. Rather than keeping my gaze on Bishop to answer his question, I turn back to Knight. Torment is clear in his features as he looks at me.

"Ask me." His brow furrows in confusion.

"Ask you what?" I steel my spine.

"Ask me who I am to Vladimir Volkov and why we survived." The edges of his eyes crinkle, narrowing to slits.

"Who the fuck are you to him, *Katarina?*" Hearing my

name, a name I haven't heard in years, roll of his tongue has a warmth spreading through me.

"I am an Antonov, I was born one and will always be one at heart." His eyes darken. "Four days after my family was executed, I became Katarina…Volkov. I am the Pakhan's wife." No sooner have the words left my mouth does chaos reign down around me. Guns are pointed in my face, each of the guys are shouting at me but I don't dare look away from the man that has somehow managed to burrow himself under my skin and demand a place inside me.

"Take her, now!" Bishop orders. I spot Luka out of the corner of my eye heading my way. I look to Knight making sure he can see it in my eyes that none of this was my choice. I never wanted this life. Luka's fingers skim my arm, he's about to grip me when Knight flies out of his chair and punches him right in the face then pulls his gun free aiming at Luka. His breaths are coming in short, rapid pants. His eyes are so dark they almost look demonic. "Put the fucking gun down, she just admitted to be the enemy, Knight."

"Bishop's right and you know it. You'll find someone else to fuck—" Knight cuts King off, pointing his gun at his brother causing the others to shout.

"You won't fucking touch her!" Knight yells. Bishop slams his fist down on the table causing me to jump.

"She is fucking dead. She is a Volkov and will fucking die—"

"She's pregnant!" Knight shouts cutting Bishop off. I stare up at him in horror. What the fuck, no. He's just saying that to save my life. I have an IUD so there is no fucking way, right?

"Oh shit."

"Fuck." I don't know who the fuck is talking. I slowly stand while keeping my gaze on Knight. He lowers his gun as he looks to me, whatever he sees in my eyes has the air rushing out of him.

"You're lying?" I don't know why I voiced it more as a question than a statement. He shakes his head. The terrified look in his eyes has bile rising in my throat. "No, no." I spin away from him ignoring the pain in my ribs and shoulder as I do and look to Bishop and King. "Kill me, kill me now." They both look horrified so I turn to Allison next. "I knew you were being held at the docks and allowed them to capture me. I needed an in to this family for protection and you were the easiest way in." Allison's face pales, I don't know why the fuck I'm admitting this shit now. I just know that what Knight says can't be true, if it is, then I'm as good as dead.

Chapter Twenty-Three

Knight

Ally slowly rises to her feet. Luka shoulders past me mumbling about me being an asshole but I ignore him. I'm too stunned by what the fuck she is doing to even focus on something else. I'm trying to save her fucking life and here she is begging my brothers to fucking kill her. What the fuck is wrong with this woman?

"Stop!" her brother yells. She whirls on him, placing both her palms on the table as she leans over.

"You know as well as I do that if what he says is true, he'll kill *it*. He'll never let me have that one fucking thing, Dimitri. Don't be so fucking dumb!" I gape at her. I've never heard her speak to him like that before, she's always been nothing but calm and caring toward her brother. Dimitri clamps his mouth closed, ducking his head to stare at his lap.

"How did you know where I was?" Ally's softly spoken question has Koby—no, Katarina turning back to her. King is at Allison's back pinning her with a look that promises pain.

"It's my fucking skillset to find things or people, everyone has one!" she screams hysterically. She's shaking, the panicked look in her eyes tells me she is about to break the fuck down. She can take being tortured and beaten but the thought of having a kid with me... unhinges her.

"I'm gonna take Mela out of here," Kiara announces as she grabs our niece and scurries from the room. King looks like he is about ready to wrap his hands around my girls neck and choke the life out of her. If he does, I'll break his fucking jaw for touching her.

"You need to calm down—"

"Oh fuck right off, Allison. Don't pretend to fucking care!" Ally's eyes fill with tears. King pushes his fiancée behind me, I dart forward and step in front of Koby shielding her from my brother.

"You really want to do this?" King's tone is low but filled with venom.

"I won't let you touch her." I make sure he can hear it in my voice that if he makes a single move, I'll fucking put him down.

"Enough!" King and I don't take our eyes off each other. "Sit the fuck down now before I beat the shit out of both you assholes." I refuse to be the one to backdown first. King clearly feels the same as I do. He pushes forward until his forehead is pushed against mine, I'm no fucking pussy so I push back against him.

He snaps and I follow, our fists fly as we plough into each other. This has been months in the making, we both knew this fight would come. Each of us has allowed our anger and frustration with the other to build. I wanted to avoid this very situation by leaving, but here we are. King tackles me to the ground landing two hits, one to my ribs and the other to my cheek. I buck my hips and roll us so I'm on top. My mind blanks as everything I have pushed down and avoided dealing with comes crashing down on me in this moment.

I take my pent up rage from Christine out on him, all the hatred toward my father unleashes, my hatred within myself for allowing my twin to be murdered comes rushing to the surface. Everything is white noise around me. I stop hitting him when he refuses to fight back, his face bloody and busted up. I pound against his chest.

"Fight back!" His eyes hold so much pain, but it's not his own, he's hurting for me. I pound my fists against his chest again. "Fucking fight back you pussy!" My voice cracks and it's only then that I realize that I'm... crying. I reach up and touch my cheek noting that the tips of my fingers are wet. I shuffle back off King and drop to my ass between his legs. He doesn't hesitate, he sits up groaning then wraps his arms around me, pulling in close. I feel Bishop crouch down beside us and rest a hand on my shoulder. I fucking lose it, wrapping my arms around my brother and clinging to him. I shut them all out because I let the guilt and shame of what I did with Christine ruin the relationship I have with my brothers. "I'm so sorry," I sob.

"Shut up. You have nothing to be sorry for." King's voice is filled with unshed tears. I clench his shirt between my hands and hold him tighter. I don't deserve his forgiveness.

"I would never have done what she asked," I choke out, needing him to know that no matter what happens between us, I would never kill my own brother! He moves his arm to grip the back of my neck, pulls me back until we are resting our foreheads against each other. His eyes shine with pride and love.

"I know." I never knew two words could hold so much power. "It wasn't your fault. You were just a kid. I'm sorry I made you feel like any of this was your fault because none of it is."

"I swear if I knew Mela was yours..."

"Shhh, I know. I know you would have told me. Mela is here now with us and that's all that matters. I need you to let this shit go, Knight. It is killing you inside. You may not want to hear it, but Bish and I won't be able to bring you back if you retreat inside yourself, that was Rook's job." At the mention of my brother, I slam my eyes closed and for the first time since he went missing I allow myself to feel the grief, the pain and the anger that accompanies any thought of him.

"You're gonna be a dad soon, kid. You need to work shit out." Bishop's tone leaves no room for argument. He's simply stating facts and he's right, I need to pull my shit together. "You dumbasses need to get cleaned up and then fix this fucking room." King and I both laugh, earning a slap on the back of each of our heads from Bishop, which just serves to make us laugh harder.

"I swear to God, boys are so stupid!" King pulls back from me and stares up at Ally who is glaring at us. He smiles sheepishly.

"Baby, words don't always work..." King clamps his mouth closed when she places her hands on her hips. She shoots her death glare to me next.

"You are such a dick. Hitting each other doesn't solve shit!" King and I share a sideways glance before busting out into fits of laughter. It feels so weird but also so good to laugh with my brother. It's not often that I laugh, if I do at all. It feels weird to hear the sound of my own laughter.

"Baby, you like it when I smack that ass so don't play coy." Bishop groans, I splutter, while Ally turns a shade of red. When a throat clears to my other side, that's when I remember we aren't alone. The light feeling inside me dies when my gaze connects with Koby's. Her green eyes are void of all emotion; her face is a blank mask. Taking a deep breath, I slowly climb to my feet and wince in pain, King got a good hit to my fucking ribs. I open my mouth to speak to her but Bish clamps a hand down on my shoulder cutting me off.

"Get cleaned up, *Katarina* and I need a moment alone." I look from him to her, noting that both of them have walled their emotions off from me. Regardless, Bishop needs to know where I stand with Koby. This situation with her isn't fucking ideal that's for sure, the one thing Bishop has raised us all knowing is that blood means everything. Neither of us may want what is coming but it's happening whether we like it or not. She's having my baby and that makes her family.

"I trust you, don't make me regret that, Bish. That's my kid in there..." She snaps her eyes to me in shock. I hold her stare as I finish speaking. "That makes her family," is all I say before I leave the room and hope to fucking god my trust in my brother isn't misplaced.

Chapter Twenty-Four

Koby

After Knight left, Bishop ushered me into his office. I'm sitting in one of the seats in front of his desk while he sits in his, behind it. The way he hasn't stopped staring at me is making me uneasy, it's like he is looking inside me and I don't know how the fuck I feel about that.

"What's your end game here?" His question doesn't exactly shock me but the fact I don't know how to answer him does. I have always had the same answer my whole life, freedom for me and my brother. "I need an answer." His tone is firm and unyielding.

"I can't give you one," I answer honestly.

"Why?" I nibble on the corner of my bottom lip unsure how to put into words what I'm thinking. I'm grateful when I hear the door open, giving me more time to think clearly on how to answer Bishop. I'm slightly taken back to see it's Kiara and Gage who entered and not Knight. She moves around the desk and drops onto Bishop's lap, placing a tender kiss to his cheek. Gage claims the chair beside me. It's funny, he looks so much like them but doesn't at the same time. Gage isn't as tightly wound as his brothers. If the information I have is correct, Gage is the third oldest in the family. "My patience is growing thin here."

I sigh before trying to voice my answer as clearly as I can to the Don. Bishop is intimidating, the guy wears three piece suits all year round and never smiles. The only reason I know the guy actually has a heart is because he is currently holding said heart against him now. Kiara Bennett has the mafia Don whipped and there is no one who can deny that.

"My aim was always to get freedom from the Bratva. I never asked for any of this or wanted any part in it. My father promised me I would never have to marry for something other than love. Vlad took that choice away when my father refused my hand in marriage." I take a deep breath and lock my emotions down, I haven't told this story in a long, long time and it still kills me to this day. "My father wasn't like other Pakhan's, he was good and cared for his people. He never had a hand in the skin trade. He said that women and children were to be treasured, not used. Vladimir didn't agree. He is the one who runs the skin trade. He is the one who will be dealing with the other families to bring in shipments."

"Your father's refusal started the war between the two

head families?" Bishop's tone isn't as harsh as it was a moment ago.

"Yes. He vowed to me I would never be used, that I could choose my own path in this life. Vladimir took that choice from me when he murdered my family. I was married to him within a week of my father's death." I can hear the anger slowly creeping into my voice as I speak of the bastard who stole everything from me.

"If you're his wife, then who is this Anya and how did you get away?" Bishop's gaze bore into me, he's watching me closely to try to detect any deceit.

"Anya and I grew up together, sort of. We became friends when we were sent to the states for school. Vlad wasn't good to her like my father was to me. She was going to be married to someone here to form an alliance. I don't know anything else about that, that is all she told me." Bishop's eyes narrow. I can see from the hard set of his jaw that this is news to him. "Once we were brought home, it was then I learned of the death of my family. I married Vlad willingly." Bishop glares at me with nothing but anger and disgust in his gaze. He opens his mouth, but Gage beats him to speak.

"He used Dimitri against you, that's why you married him without a fuss." I don't take my eyes off Bishop as I nod. My agreement seems to ease some of the tension in the Don's body.

"What happened next?" Bishop is pushing for his answers and I truly don't blame him.

"We stayed until I was nearly nineteen. Anya was the one who helped us escape her father. I didn't ask any details or look a gift horse in the mouth. I took the tickets and ran.

We had new identities and a chance at a life that didn't involve being raped daily by your best friend's father." Kiara flinches in Bishop's hold, he tightens his hold around her and pulls her in closer.

"What else?" A whoosh of air rushes out of me at his question.

"Dimitri and I landed in the states. We ran for months until we were sure we weren't being followed. I made money fighting in each city we passed by until we hit New York. I got a message from Anya saying that a family here had caused trouble for her father. I thought what better place to hide out, than right under his nose with his enemies."

"How did you know about Allison?" Gage asks. I nibble on my lip debating if I should answer or not. In the end I decide I've told them everything so far so I may as well continue on.

"St Mary's isn't like most schools... it teaches you to fight, shoot, kill, hack. They even teach you how to be a good housewife and block out pain in case your husband decides to share you with his buddies."

"Where the fuck is that school?" Kiara demands. I smile wickedly at the girl as I answer.

"I burnt that bitch to the ground when I came back. It's nothing but a pile of ashes now." She nods and returns my smile.

"Atta girl." She beams, I can see the vengeance in her eyes. Kiara is a rarity. She isn't a spoiled brat or accepts anything from anyone. She genuinely cares about people and only wants to help them.

"So, you learnt how to track from a... school?" I nod in answer to Gage's question.

"I'm not sold. There is more to this and I want the full story." Bishop is good, just from looking at me he can tell I'm holding back.

"I looked into each of you when Anya told me about your family. I tracked everyone from each of your pasts, knew about the secrets your family thought they had buried. I'm good at what I do. Do you really think Knight found out what he did about me without me knowing?" Bishop grits his teeth in anger. "I allowed him and Luka to find things out, I knew it was the only way to buy me time until I could get out. You want a hacker, then I'm the person for the job. I can have every cent from Pauly and Vinny's accounts wired into an offshore account that can't be traced."

"How long were you going to play my brother?" I feel like he punched me in the gut, the accusation clear in his tone. He thinks because everything else I have done was a ploy for my freedom that must mean I was playing with his brother's head.

"The plan was to wait for you to take out Vlad, then Dimitri and I would run, meet up with Anya and finally be free."

"What changed?" This time it's Kiara who asks me a question. I mull over my words for a moment before deciding to just speak the fucking truth.

"Knight. He changed everything. I don't know how it happened but he went from being the guy who was in the shadows watching me to becoming... my dark Knight." I shrug my shoulders unsure how else I can explain how I feel about him.

"Do you still plan to run from him?" I hold Kiara's gaze as I answer her question.

"I don't want to, but if what he says is true and Vlad finds out about this baby, he won't stop." Bishop's eyes harden.

"You run with his baby and he'll hunt you down. We'll all hunt you down—" I cut Bishop off, he doesn't get it.

"If I stay here, I not only put the fucking baby in danger, I put him in danger! Vladimir will torture him slowly and make me watch, then he'll make me watch as he kills my child. I got an IUD in secret so I would never carry an heir for Vlad. Anya is his only child but she isn't a male. I never fucking wanted children!" I yell.

"Then don't." I'm on my feet and spin around to find Knight leaning against the wall with his arms crossed over his chest.

"H-how long have you been there?" I ask.

Chapter Twenty-Five

Knight

I can see I've shocked her. I've been here the whole time since Kiara and Gage walked in. I didn't want her to know I was here. I needed her to speak freely so I could gauge her intentions and so far, she hasn't disappointed me.

"Long enough to know that you aren't our... my enemy." Her shoulders visibly relax at my words.

"I can't have this baby." I stiffen but make sure to keep my face blank of all emotions. I look to Bishop instead of answering her.

"You satisfied?" He cuts his gaze between me and Koby before sighing.

"Not in the fucking least, but I also know killing her

would kill you, so what the fuck do I do?" I fight the smirk that wants to break free.

"You trust me, trust that I know she isn't bad. If she was, she would have killed me a long time ago and helped the Russians at the dock." That seems to appease him a little. He taps Kiara to hop off, they both stand and Gage follows their lead.

"Koby?" She slowly pulls her gaze from me to look at Bishop. "I don't trust you, probably never will either." She nods her head. "As long as that baby is inside you, you have my word that my family will allow no harm to come to you or that child." She nods again. Bishop's eyes darken and I ready myself for him to lay it out for her. "You try to run with that baby and believe me, I will kill you with my bare hands. You want your freedom, you can have it." I open my mouth to tell him to fuck off but he pushes on. "But after the child is born, only then will I allow you your freedom."

"You so much as try to take this baby from me and I'll burn this fucking house down with you all in it." Bishop laughs but there is no humor to it.

"Be glad you don't have a dick."

"Why?" Koby asks, confused by Bish's statement.

"Because if you did, I would have knocked your teeth down your throat." He doesn't say another word as he leads Kiara and Gage from the room. Koby and I stand here staring at each other. I don't know what the fuck to say to her. Do I care about her... yeah, I fucking do. Do I want this baby? Yeah, I fucking do. I never thought a girl and a kid would be in the cards for me but shit changes. Now I need her and this baby more then I need my next breath. I need her beside me daily. She was the only thing keeping the nightmares at bay. I didn't know I even had feelings for her until losing her became a possibility.

"He'll kill you," she whispers.

"Let him try."

"This isn't a joke, Knight."

"Never said it was." She rests her ass on the edge of Bishop's desk. I hate the space between us, so I close it. I gently grip her thighs and lift her so she can sit on top of his desk. I stand between her legs and stare down at her, seeing a war of emotions swirling in her eyes.

"You tortured me."

"You lied to me," I defend.

"You fucking locked me in a dungeon!" I cringe. That is something I will spend the rest of my life hating myself for.

"I lost my best friend, Koby. I wasn't thinking straight. Fuck, I'm still not thinking straight." She reaches up and rests her palms flat against my chest.

"How do you know I'm pregnant?" I fill her in about what happened with doc and him testing her blood.

"But I have an IUD, I can't get pregnant." Her argument is weak, even I know those things can fall out if a chick has a heavy period or something like that. "I can't be a mom." I cup her face between my hands and lean down resting my head against hers.

"I'm not cut out to be a dad either. Fuck, I never wanted a kid but now that it's here, I want it so badly, Koby."

"This child won't be our savior, Knight. It won't right our wrongs. We are bringing a child into this world in the middle of a war, which by the way I will not sit back and not fight!" Now that fucks me right off.

"Like fuck. Your ass will be staying right fucking here—"

"Hell no, I'm an asset—"

"You're pregnant with my kid!"

"Our kid!" Hearing those two words out of her mouth has a smile splitting my face. Before I even know what I'm doing, I have my lips sealed to her demanding entrance. She opens for me and I moan at the taste of her. Koby is a fucking addiction I wasn't willing to admit I had. She is a drug that runs through my veins. I know now, as I stand here nestled between her legs and kissing her, that I've... fallen for her.

Three weeks later....

Koby is finally able to breathe easier and actually move without difficulty. The doc is coming to take her stitches out today. There is still tension between her and my brothers. The girls have tried to make it up to her and apologize about not helping her, but Koby is stubborn as fuck. I can't deal with all of that shit and still continue to search for my brother. Bishop wanted to call Car and fill her in on what happened, but I stopped him. I need to be the one to tell our sister about Rook. We have all agreed no service, wake or funeral will be held for him because none of us believe he is truly gone. He can't be!

"Knight?" I turn around to find Dimitri standing in the doorway. I've been staying out in the guest house with him and Koby. The tension inside the house with Koby and the others does my fucking head in. I don't have the energy to sort that shit and she has threatened my balls if I do. I put my phone in my pocket and decide to call my sister later. Honestly, I'm dreading calling her. Her and Rook were always really close growing up, so I know the news is going break her.

"What's up?"

"The doctor is here and asked to see you." Shit. I shove past him and rush into the living room thinking something is wrong with Koby but freeze when I see her shirt pulled up to just under her boobs and the doctor moving a wand thing around on her stomach. A throat clears drawing my attention to just behind the couch, I'm fucking shocked to see my brothers and both the girls standing there. Koby is laying on the couch, stiff as shit and looking so out of her comfort zone. Each of them smiles reassuringly at me. I turn to Koby to find her eyes on me, she looks fucking terrified. She lifts her hand using her index finger to call me, and as if I'm on autopilot, I do as she says and walk over to her. I kneel down beside her head and cradle her face. The doc turns and smiles like this situation is normal.

Nothing about this is normal. The woman who is carrying my child is married to the boss of the family we are at war with. I've had a couple weeks to come to terms with all of this, but it's hard. Koby and I have coexisted but haven't pushed the line. It's not through my lack of trying. I want to fuck her to get rid of the sexual tension pulsing between us.

"Congratulations. You're around six weeks and both babies have a strong heartbeat."

"Both?" Koby and I say in unison. The Doctor looks

between the both of us before pushing his lips to the side and jerking his head in a nod.

"Yes, both. As in you are having twins."

Jesus fucking Christ!

Chapter Twenty-Six

Koby

I sit on the edge of the pool with my feet dangling in the water gazing up at the night sky. So many stars shine brightly tonight. I feel like the universe is playing a cruel joke on me—I get the worst possible news today but then a stunning night as if to ease the sting.

Twins!

How is that even possible for him to fucking get me twice. The Doc says identical twins. Knight took off after hearing that. I want to be pissed as hell at him, but I get it. He lost his twin and now finds out he is about to be a father to not just any twins but identical ones like him and Rook. Once he took off, I kicked the Doc and everyone else out. I didn't need their prying or pity, I just needed some fucking time to process shit! How the fuck has my life turned out like this?

The first guy that makes me feel something and I manage to fall pregnant by him. Killing Vlad isn't just about my freedom now, it's the life—lives I carry inside me. I lay my hand against my flat stomach and just... feel them. I never wanted this, I had no intentions of ever having children but now that they are here and are real... I want them. Even if their father doesn't, I'll love them enough for the both of us so they will never have to wonder what the love of a father feels like. I sit forward, dropping my hand to my side as I stare down at my stomach. For the first time since finding out I was pregnant, I feel something other than dread.

"You... both of you may have been unplanned," I say quietly to my stomach. "I don't know what to say really... but I want to promise you both something. I will give you everything I can, be the best mom I can. I will never let the darkness of this world or the life I have lived touch either of you... I'll... love you both with all of me." I feel a lone tear slide down my cheek. I don't swipe it away, it actually brings a smile to my face to know I'm still able to feel these types of emotions. Crying was something Vlad or my teachers never allowed us to show, it's seen as a sign of weakness. Just thinking about Vladimir has my heart racing. No matter how hard you try to hide things, they always have a way of getting out, just like this pregnancy will. When he finds out, he will kill Knight and make me watch.

"I promise..." I turn to peer over my shoulder, already sensing him near before he spoke, his dark silhouette leaning against the side of the house. He pushes off and slowly stalks toward me with a swagger only Knight Murdoch could pull off. He drops down beside me not caring that his shoes get wet in the pool water. He reaches out to brush his knuckles softly against my cheek, his eyes are full of wonder and... lust. "To love both of them with everything I have. I also promise to take care of you and our children." I hear the truth in his words. I'm going to blame the whole pregnancy hormones for the tears that cloud my eyes, because I do not cry!

"Just because we are having... kids together don't mean anything, Knight. You're barely eighteen and have a life ahead of you." His eyes darken but I need to get this out. "I don't expect anything from you, never have and never will. My life is fucked up and I can't promise you forever. I'm not the type of girl that dreams of a white picket fence or a wedding. I'm the girl that fights to survive, kills or be killed. That is me and I won't change, I can't." He wraps his hand around the back of my neck and tightens his hold to the point of pain before he yanks me in close and bends so there is only a sliver of space between us. His breaths come in short rapid pants, his eyes shining with contempt.

"You listen to me and listen fucking good. I've grown up faster than any man my age. I didn't get the childhood or freedom like the rest of these pansy bitches around town. I know what I want, Koby."

"What exactly do you want, Knight?" I whisper, hating that hope surges inside me that he will say the words I need to hear him say. Knight is not someone you can recover from. Broken hearts heal over time but he is so much more. He burrows himself so deep inside you that you don't even realize he is a part of you until it's too late.

"You." One word, that's all it takes for him to shatter every wall I have built up over my lifetime. I've never wanted anything as much as I want him and in equal parts it terrifies the fuck out of me and excites the shit out of me. "Give me all of you, Koby. Everything you have to offer and I promise you, every part of me will belong to only you." The air rushes from my lungs, the sincerity in his gaze tells me he means every word.

"Loving you will destroy me, you know that, right?" A cocky smirk lifts on one side.

"Loving you has awoken parts of me I thought died a really long time ago." My eyes widen in surprise which just turns his smirk into a full-blown smile, the cocky bastard knows exactly what he has done.

"Y-you love me?" His eyes close for a moment. I can see pain etched across his beautiful face, my own heart aches for him. I know he has been through some fucked up shit with King's ex, if the bitch wasn't dead already, I'd kill her. What Knight and I have between us isn't conventual at all, I mean the guy tied me up and tortured me for fuck's sake and yet, here I am hanging onto every fucking word he says. He drops his hand to his lap and tilts his head back to look up at the night sky as he speaks.

"I thought I knew what love was, I mean I love my siblings but I love... Rook more than any of them." He chuckles but there isn't humor to it, only pain. "I thought I found a different type of love when Christine came along. She was different from the other girls. She paid attention to me. Made me feel... good. She played with my head so good, it made me think she actually loved me. Shit, I thought I loved her." A whoosh of air escapes him before he continues. "She wanted me to kill King, told me if I did it we could be together forever."

"She's a fucking bitch for even thinking to ask you to do that." A strained laugh comes from him, but I can see the pain in his eyes.

"I fucked up so badly, Koby. The thought of loving her made me do some fucked up shit. I was fucking my brother's girlfriend—the mother of his child—and I never felt an ounce of remorse until she asked me to take him out. As fucked up as I am, even I knew she had crossed a line."

"Why are you telling me this?" I whisper as I move my feet back and forth through the water. I keep my gaze straight ahead, I can feel his intense gaze boring into the side of my head.

"Because what I feel for you is more than I ever felt for her. I feel you inside me ,Koby. I can find you in a room crowded with people because there is a tether that pulls me to you." I slowly turn to him, his eyes are bright and I can see it in the depths of his gaze that a weight has been removed from his shoulders. "I'm not like the others. I don't do this talking shit. I've never had a girlfriend because I don't do commitment, but I want to try with you."

"Because of the babies?" I hold my breath waiting for him to answer, praying he says what I need him to in order for me to finally be able to let him. He reaches out and brushes his thumb across my check as he searches my gaze.

"No, I wanted to try with you before I even knew they existed." I smack his hand away and pull him to me so I can kiss him. He stiffens for a second before he wises up and takes control. He fists my hair in his hand and deepens the kiss, drawing a moan from me. He pulls back and jumps to his feet not caring that his shoes or the bottoms of his jeans are soaking wet. He reaches for me and I don't fight, allowing him to lift me from the pool. I wrap my arms and legs around him and stare into his eyes, wondering how the fuck I got here.

I never thought that feeling the way I do about him, or even having the smallest amount of hope for the future, would be something I was ever blessed with. Knight is opening up parts of me I thought I had died along with my family. This crazy boy is giving me hope that I won't just have to live day to day.

My dark Knight is making me see clearly for the first time in years.

Chapter Twenty-Seven

Knight

I walk us back toward the guest house and don't stop until we reach her room. Kicking the door shut, I place her gently on her feet. I may have just said some soppy shit that I will never say again, and I did mean every word of it, but now, I need to fuck the shit out of my girl so she knows who the fuck she belongs to. I wrap my hand around the back of her neck, forcing her to tilt her head up so she can meet my stare. When I see the longing in her eyes I know I have her, she's mine.

"We do this, this is it for us. You belong to me, Koby." I place my free hand against her flat stomach, and a gasp spills from her plump lips. "These are mine, my blood, my future. You fuck me over, Koby, or try to flee from me with my kids and I promise you, next time I tie you to a chair you won't see the light of day again."

She reaches up, laying her hands flat against my pecs. I narrow my eyes. Koby may look like an innocent blonde that can be toyed with but I know fucking better. This crazy girl could kill you with a fucking pen! Her green eyes hold my stare as she slowly runs her hands down my abs and stops at the waistband of my jeans.

"I hear everything you said, every last word." Her eyes sharpen and her features pull taut. "Now you listen to me. You so much as allow another woman to touch you, or you make fuck me eyes at anyone aside from me, I'll tie your ass to the back of your own car and drag you past your family. Then I'll reverse over you just make sure your fucking dead." I fight the smile that wants to break free. "You fuck me over, Knight, and I swear to you on the lives of our children, I'll show you what it is like to be tortured by a Bratva heiress. Be warned, we Russian's show no mercy."

I'm so fucking hard for her right now!

I slam my lips to hers and show her with this kiss that I own her as much as she owns me. I'll fight for her. I'll fight for us. I won't fucking let her husband take her from me. With that thought, I break the kiss and fight the laugh that wants to tear from me at the angry look she shoots me.

"I'm done talking, playboy!" she growls.

"You're getting a divorce." Her eyes widen and her mouth opens, but I push on. "Don't fucking fight me. I'm getting the papers sorted now and you will sign the fucking dotted line, Koby." Her eyes search mine and it stuns me when I see tears cloud her vision.

"I'll be an Antonov again?" I bit back the growl that wants to tear from me and speak.

"Yes."

But not for long, I think to myself as I reach for her shirt and lift it over her head. I leave her bra on as I help her out of her pants. She stands before me in a matching purple bra and thong, this girl has a body to fucking die for. She reaches for me but I step back. I want a few more seconds to enjoy my view. Her stomach is still flat but I know as days turn to weeks her belly will grow with my children. I drop to my knees in front of her and slowly peel her thong down her long legs, relishing in the shiver that rolls through her body as my finger skim her thighs. I lock my gaze onto hers as I lift her leg and place it over my shoulder bringing her pussy in line with my face. The scent of her invades me and I growl as I tear my gaze from hers to feast my eyes on her bare, glistening pussy.

My mouth waters at the sight of it. I dart my tongue out to swipe through her slick folds, earning a sharp cry from her. I need her to come on my face, I need to see the blissed-out look in her eyes as I drive my cock deep inside her tight little body. I grip the globes of her ass and pull her flush against my face as I feast on her cunt. Pushing my tongue inside her tight wet hole, I relish in the sounds that tear from her. She rides my face chasing her release, a release only I can give her.

"Oh fuck, yes, don't stop." I flatten my tongue against her clit and apply enough pressure to send her over the edge. Her leg locks around me as her hand clamps down on the back of my head holding me in place as she shatters above me. I don't give her time to come down slowly, I push her leg off and make quick work of stripping off. Her eyes are dazed as they run the length of my body, my cock jutting against my stomach proudly. I reach for her, gripping the backs of her thighs. She locks her legs around me and rests her hands on my shoulders as she leans down to capture my lips. She moans at the taste of herself, the sound has my cock twitching against her ass.

I move us until she is flush against the wall. Reaching between our bodies, I line my cock up with her entrance and slam inside her. She throws her head back and moans, I groan at the feeling of her pussy walls clenching the fuck out of my cock, milking it already. Unable to remain still, I begin to move inside her. Reaching up, I rip the cups of her bra down and latch onto her right nipple. She screams as I bite down on it before switching sides to do the same to the other. My thrusts begin to grow erratic as I chase my own release.

"I'm close, baby. I need you to get there." Her eyes are unfocused as she cups my face and stares down at me.

"Fuck me hard and make me feel you between my legs tomorrow."

Her wish is my command.

I fuck her hard. I'm so deep inside her that I never want to leave her body. She screams my name as she comes all over my cock. I'm two seconds away from blowing so I pull out of her and shove her to knees. I grip my cock in my hand pumping it fast, the she devil in front of me opens her mouth taunting me. The sight of her naked and on her knees waiting for my cum has me exploding. I come with her name on my lips. I watch as jets of my cum lands on her chest, face and in her mouth. She swallows me and moans at the taste. This girl is fucking perfection.

Waking up this morning sucked. I didn't want to leave Koby but I also knew Bishop would kick my ass if I didn't meet with him this morning. I don't bother knocking as I push open his office door and fucking freeze. Kiara is spread out over his desk with her dress bunched around her waist and Bishop's face between her legs.

"Fuck." Bishop lifts his gaze to mine. Anger swells in the depths of his eyes, so before he can yell and scream, I pull the door shut and make my way into the kitchen laughing.

"You walked in, didn't you?" I meet King's gaze over the counter and nod. The fucker laughs, causing me to follow suit. "He is going to kick your ass." I shrug my shoulders and head for the coffee pot.

"Fucker should learn to lock the fucking door then." Gage walks in at that moment with Ally at his side. It used to bother King how close Ally had grown to me, Rook and Gage but he sees now that she may love us, but not in the way she loves him. Allison would die for King and their daughter in a heartbeat. Speaking of, Meelz runs past her mom and straight for me. I bend down and scoop her up, holding her close. She places a wet kiss to my cheek and grins at me.

"Missed you, Uncle Right." I smile sadly at her. I have pulled away from my niece since shit with her dad blew up, and I'm an asshole for doing that.

"I missed you too."

"Where's Uncle Cook?" Her innocent question has a pang shooting straight through my chest. As if she can sense it, Ally makes her way over to me. She reaches out for her daughter, who goes willingly, then grips my forearm, giving it a gentle squeeze.

"We're all here for you, whatever you need." Unable to speak, I just nod my thanks. Ally has always been able to see through the bullshit mask I wear. It's unnerving that I can't hide from her.

"So you meeting with Bish?" King and I both share a loaded look before turning back to Gage and laughing. His face is laced with confusion. "What?"

"Uh, the big guy is a bit busy getting relieved..." King lets his sentence trail off not wanting to say anymore with his daughter in the room. Once Gage catches on his face scrunches up in disgust.

"That's nasty," he sneers.

"You hit that first," I blurt, making Gage's eyes widen. King looks worried... for me? When he flicks his gaze past me, I cringe and slowly turn to see Bishop and Kiara standing in the doorway. The princess is trying hard not to laugh, my brother, on the other hand, looks like he wants to beat the shit out of me.

"Say that shit again and I'll break your fucking neck, asshole." The threat in his voice is clear. Bishop doesn't fuck around when it comes to Kiara.

"Then you best be helping me with these babies if he's dead." All eyes swing toward the backdoor where Koby and Dimitri just entered. I smirk at my little killer as she saunters across the room. I expect her to beeline for me but the smile vanishes from my face when she stops next to fucking Gage!

Chapter Twenty-Eight

Koby

I pull my gaze from Gage when King's booming laughter sounds out. Allison stands next to him glaring at his hunched over form. He's pointing to Knight. I turn to him and find an angry scowl on his face directed at Gage. I'm about to ask what his problem is when a deep rumble comes from Bishop, it shocks the shit out of me to see the big man laughing. Kiara smacks him on the chest, shaking her head.

"Feel the fucking burn like we do, asshole," King wheezes out between laughter. Knight looks between his two brothers and for the first time since meeting him, I see some of the tension he carries on a daily basis lessen. A small smile curves his lips as he shakes his head and smacks

King's hand away. He stalks toward me, wraps an arm around my shoulder and pulls me away from Gage.

"Get your own fucking girl," he bites out as he leads me toward the dining table with the other's laughter following after us.

Sitting here eating breakfast with all of them feels... nice. For the first time there isn't any tension. I look to the side to see Knight's gaze focused in front of him to the empty chair—Rook's chair. My heart hurts for him and I wish I could help him through this, but he won't be able to move on from this unless they find the body. I reach over and place my hand on top of his thigh offering my silent support. His gaze swings to me instantly, the corners of his eyes etched with concern. I smile and hope he can see it in my eyes that I'm here for him—

My train of thought is cut off when Mav and Luka come bounding into the room.

"Boss." Bishop is up out of his seat and moving toward his guys in an instant.

"What is it?" The power that radiates off Bishop is awe inspiring. Each of these Murdoch men give off a different vibe. Rook is playful and caring, King is silent and deadly, Gage is... I don't know what he is but Knight, he's a silent killer. The vibe he gives off is cold and callous when in truth, out of each of his brothers, I can tell he is the one that loves the hardest because he is the hardest out of them all to get close to.

"Pauly and AJ made a move," Luka rushes to say.

"What'd they do?" Bishop growls whilst clenching his fists at his sides.

"They tried to buy out the silent partners in California.

They're coming after the income and then for you." Bishop nods mulling over Mav's words, but before he can speak Gage pipes up.

"And how is it that you found this out before it happened, Mav?" All eyes cut to Gage. Mav doesn't even flinch under the pressure of Gage's gaze.

"It's my job to know." The anger that laces Mav's words makes it clear he and Gage don't like each other.

"Set it up. Get the guys together and set Knight up a fight for tomorrow night. He'll draw AJ out and we'll make a move on Pauly. We end this shit with them and then go after Vinny. I want each of my brother's running their territories and their men under us, then we go for the Bratva."

"If we do that, we should have enough soldiers to go after the Russian's—" I cut King off.

"No." All eyes swing to me. I keep my eyes on Bishop as I continue. "Vlad has the local police, armies and his men at his disposal. You will need more than what you will have to go against him. If you want him out..." I turn to Knight as I say the last part. "I'll draw him out." Knight's eyes darken.

"You're out your fucking mind if you think that is an option." His tone is low but his words hold the weight of his rage.

"It might be the only way—" Knight cuts his stare to Bishop, who clamps his mouth closed.

"You find another way. She isn't going to be the bait. I won't lose some—I won't let her do it." My heart aches for him, he's terrified of losing someone else he loves.

After breakfast all the guys retreated to Bishop's office to hash out a plan. I thought I would be spending the day hacking to try find Anya. She hasn't checked in. Kiara and Allison asked if I would go to the gym with them and honestly, I jumped at the chance to get the fuck out of here and clear my mind. The gym seems to be the only place I can do that.

The car ride is silent but it's not uncomfortable. I don't have anything against either of these two. I actually like them both and for the first time I allow myself the freedom to actually get to know them instead of closing myself off and preparing to run. Liking people and creating connections makes shit difficult when you have to drop everything and run in an instant.

"So, you and Knight huh." I snort while Kiara laughs at Ally's attempt to spark a conversation. She narrows her gaze on Kiara who just shrugs her shoulders whilst keeping her eyes on the road. Ally peers over her seat and looks at me expectantly. I can't help the stupid smile that spreads across my face.

"Yeah," I breathe out. They each ask me questions about mine and Knight's relationships as we drive to the gym.

"I'm so glad he finally let someone in, he's going to need you when the search..." Kiara clamps her mouth closed, not daring to speak her thoughts aloud. We're all thinking it, but no one has said it. Rook is dead but the guys won't acknowledge that. "Has he said anything to you about how he's coping?" An irrational sense of pride swells inside me knowing he hasn't spoken to either of these two, only me.

"He won't give up on him, he can't. It's not in his make

up," is I all say before climbing out of the car once Kiara parks out the front of the gym. Once inside, I head straight for the locker rooms to change and get ready to lose myself in a workout. I need to clear my mind and try to sort out everything that is swirling inside my head. Anya hasn't checked in—she has never missed a check in with me. I'm pregnant. Dimitri seems to be coming out of shell more. Knight... we are a thing. Just the thought of him has me fighting to keep the smile from my face.

I'm in the ring with Gage, who showed up at the gym about twenty minutes after us. He's been running the three of us through a workout that has my muscles aching but in the best possible way. My ribs are healed so I'm not in pain, but the wound that is almost healed on my shoulder gives me a bit of grief but I push through it.

"Bend your knees, Ally. Hands up, doll." Gage turns to me and motions for me to join him in the center. I do. I get into position and wait for him to tell me what's next. He places his hands on my hips ready to give instructions but freezes when we hear a gun cock. All of us turn toward the entrance and freeze.

Bishop stands in the middle with his glare pointed at his girl. King to his right with an unreadable expression on his face. I look to Bishop's left to find Knight's gaze already on me, no not on me exactly, he's eyeing Gage's hands on me. I step out of Gage's hold and grit my teeth. I am not doing this shit.

Chapter Twenty-Nine

Knight

I watch as she pulls out of Gage's hold, jumps from the ring and heads for the locker room. I chase after her, there is no fucking way this shit is going to keep happening! I kick the door open causing it to slam against the wall with a resounding bang. I walk to the second row of lockers and stop when I see her peeling her Spanx down her legs. I cross my arms over my chest and lean against the locker, she narrows her eyes but doesn't stop. She peels her crop top off and stands before me in a thong and white sports bra.

"Say whatever it is you have to say, don't be a pussy," she grits out as she grabs a towel from the locker. Oh hell, fucking no. I grip her arm as she tries to walk past and glare down at her.

"There is no fucking way you are showering here." She pulls free of my hold and pushes her lips to the side before shaking her head and marching her naked ass to the shower. Growling I stalk after her. She has just turns the water on, then I'm crowding her space. She moves until her back is against the cold, tiled wall, and hisses when her back touches the wall. Jerking forward, I push into her keeping her in place with my body. I use my arms to cage her in, not giving a fuck that I'm getting soaked from the shower head.

"What is your problem?" she snaps. I drop my arms from either side of her head and grip the globes of her ass, causing her to gasp and lurch forward so she is flush against me.

"This is mine," I growl as I knead her cheeks. Her eyes glaze over with need. "I'm the only one who gets to see this ass, not Gage or any other fucker that comes here." I move one of my hands and push between our bodies to cup her sex, she moans then quickly bites her lip. "This is mine, Katarina, no one else gets to see this but me." She gasps at the use of her real name and tips her head to the side offering me her neck.

"Then take what's yours, playboy." Her voice is raspy and full of need. I free myself from my jeans and lift her. She locks her legs around my waist and smashes her lips against mine. I push her thong to the slide and run a finger through her slit making sure she is ready for me, groaning when I feel her arousal coat my finger.

"You're fucking soaked for me, baby." Her only response is to moan and grind down against my finger. I pull it out before it can slip inside her tight wet cunt. She groans in annoyance. I line my cock up and prod at her entrance.

She tries to push down but I hold her still. "You don't change here, shower here or anything. This is your last training session at this gym." She opens her mouth to argue, so I slam inside her to disrupt her train of thought.

"Fuck, Knight!" I lean forward and bite the side of her neck, slamming into her at a punishing rate. I can feel her clenching my cock ready to come, so I pull back. I do this twice before she growls. "What the fuck?" I pull back from her neck and glare down at her.

"Agree to my terms and I'll let you come, baby, I'll let you come all over my cock." Her pupils dilate then narrow, before she can argue I push inside her again distracting her with my dick. "Agree, baby, and I'll let you come." I see the fight in her eyes, she wants to tell me to fuck off but she also needs this release.

"Knight—" I slam my mouth against hers and kiss her, pouring all my emotions into this kiss hoping she can feel what I feel for her. She turns her face to the side, breaking the kiss. She cups my face between her hands, her gaze searching mine for a moment. "I won't stop training…" I'm prepared to argue but she pushes on. "But I'll train at the gym at your house." A satisfied smirk graces my face in triumphant. "Now fuck me and make me scream your name, playboy." I do just that, I fuck her hard and fast until we both come harder then we have before crying out the others name.

Koby and I make our way out of the locker room. I ignore my brothers and the girls' laughter, pulling Koby closer into my side. Koby laughs along with the others and within a second I join them. I'm fucking soaked from head to toe and without a doubt, they all know we were in the back fucking. Plus, they probably heard Koby screaming my name.

———

"Will we stay here?" I pull my gaze from my laptop and look to Dimitri who is sitting on the couch opposite me. Koby and I came home and hung out at the guest house all day—fucking and... laughing. It's been a day I'll never forget, that's for sure.

"Yeah, bro, you both will live here." It's strange to sit here and watch a fifteen year old boy lose the weight of the world from his shoulders. Koby has tried to shield him from all the horrors she has had to face, but always being on the run and never having a place to call home, no school or anything must be hard for the kid. That's when the idea hits me. "How would you feel about going to school?" His eyes widen in surprise, a huge smile graces his face.

"Yes——"

"Het!" (No.) Dimitri's shoulders fall at Koby's one word.

"Why not?" I shock the shit out of myself asking that question. Believe it or not, I've grown to actually like the kid a bit. Her green eyes swing to me and narrow in warning.

"He can't——"

"Why not?" She ducks her gaze to the floor in shame.

"He hasn't been in years," she whispers. I stand and drop my laptop in the seat I was just on, before moving toward her, wrapping my arms around her and bury my nose in her hair, inhaling her scent.

"He needs this, baby. I'll get him tutors and whatever

else he will need to get him up to speed with kids his own age." She pulls back and stares up at me with tears in her eyes.

"You'd do that for him?" I smile.

"I'd do that for you and our family." A lone tear slips down her cheek. I reach up and brush it away with my thumb and place a kiss to her lips before stepping back to allow her time alone with her brother. I step out and let them talk for a bit. I have a brother of my own to search for.

Chapter Thirty

Koby

It's the night of the fight and my nerves are going crazy. Bishop had to change plans and push the fight ahead two weeks' time because he and Kiara had to fly to Miami to see her father. Knight's in his own head and I don't know how to pull him out. As the days pass, I know he is trying to hold on and not recede inside himself. Every day he is on his laptop, hacking every camera near the dock trying to find a sign that his brother is alive. It breaks my heart every night when he crawls into bed beside me and I see the defeated look in his eyes. He needs this fight to use as an outlet.

"What the hell do you think you're doing?" I meet his

gaze in the bathroom mirror as I finish tying my hair in a high ponytail. I slowly turn to face him. He runs his gaze over me. I'm wearing black, knee-high boots, tight black jeans, a white off the shoulder top and decided to apply a bit of makeup.

"Getting ready to leave?" His eyes crinkle at the corners.

"You're not coming, end of discussion." He turns and flees. I chase after him because there is no fucking way he is telling me what I can and can't do. He opens the door and races from the guest house, I'm hot on his heels.

"If you keep fucking walking away from me, playboy, I'll kick your fucking ass!" He slams to a stop in the middle of the lawn then swings around to face me. I hold his heated stare as I place my hands on my hips. "What is your problem?"

"Go back inside, baby. Your ass isn't coming with me." I scowl up at the controlling bastard.

"I'm coming. You can either bring me with you or I'll call Gage and get him—" The words die in my throat as he darts forward crowding my space. He grips the back of my neck, hauls me against him, then bends at the knees so we are eye level. The intensity in his gaze sends a shiver down my spine.

"Say his fucking name again, baby, and your pussy will pay the price." My mouth drops open in shock. He uses his free hand to push my mouth closed. I smack it away. "If you keep your mouth open like that, I'll take it as an invitation to fill it."

"If you don't take me with you, then your cock will never see the inside of my pussy again," I sass back. His eyes darken, he loves it when I fight back he just won't admit it.

"I can't, you have to stay here."

"Why?" He sighs before dropping his forehead to mine.

"I won't be able to focus on the fight or what happens after if you're in the crowd." He places his hand on my stomach like he does at least a dozen times a day making me smile. "I can't risk you getting hurt or something happening to our babies. Please, don't fight me on this." I can hear the plea in his tone and as much as I want to tell him to kiss my ass, I don't. I wrap my arms around his waist and rest my cheek against his chest breathing him in. This right here is the reason I never wanted to care. I hate that I can't control what is going to happen. Losing him would break me.

I pull back keeping my hands on his waist as I search his gaze, all I see is love shinning back at me and it steals the fucking breath from my lungs. I run my hands up his sides wrapping them around his neck, I pull him to me and kiss him. The taste of him invades my senses and I moan, he pulls back before I can go any further and rests his forehead against mine. I keep my eyes closed as I whisper.

"I love you." Three simple words that I have never spoken aloud, not even to my own brother. Voicing those words aloud means you are giving someone else a power over you that they can use to destroy you. I just gave Knight Murdoch the power to obliterate me. Tension begins to coil inside me at the fact he hasn't uttered a single word. I try to pull back but he tightens his arms around me, holding me in place. His eyes remain closed as he speaks.

"Say it again." His voice is barely above a whisper. I hear a voice coming from behind him and know that the time has come for him to leave with his brother and end another family. I say it again because even if he doesn't feel the same way, I need him to remain focused and come back to me.

"I love you." His eyes snap open, a huge smile spreads across his handsome face.

"I love you too—"

"Knight, time to go," King shouts, cutting him off. He sighs before placing a kiss to my lips, then dropping to his knees in front of me. He lays both his hands flat against my stomach and places a kiss to my belly. I look up to see the Bishop, King, Kiara, Ally, Gage and a few others standing around watching us. Both girls grips onto their men and stare without a care in the world.

"Look after your momma. I promise, I'll be back." His voice is barely above a whisper but I catch it. "You two are my redemption." Tears cloud my eyes as he stands and stalks off toward his brothers without so much as a backward glance. Bishop claps him on the shoulder as he passes. I stiffen when Bishop and King make their way toward me. Knight spins around ready to follow but both girls and Gage stop him. The torn look on his face breaks my heart, so I fake a smile and nod, letting him know I'm okay.

Bishop and King stand before me with only a couple feet of space between us. King wears all black while Bishop is in his normal three piece suit, except his suit and tie is all black. They each run their gazes over me. I keep my head held high and stand tall. I don't give a fuck what they think of me, it isn't their dicks I'm riding at the end of each night.

"I had my doubts about you," King grunts. I keep my mouth closed and wait for them to say whatever it is they came to say. "Turns out... I was wrong." That has me reeling back in shock and he shoots me a half smirk.

"How so?" I ask. Bishop grunts drawing my attention to him.

"I know you have been the one hacking Pauly and Vinny's accounts—" I open my mouth but he raises a hand silencing me. "You may have sent the information from Knight's computer but I know how my brother types... That lazy little fucker doesn't use punctuation, but you do." I push my tongue against my cheek not wanting to lie. "Why?" I peer around him to see Knight is now being held back by Gage and three others. I smile sadly at him before facing his two brothers and speaking the truth.

"Because he is important to me and I know you are important to him. I'll do whatever I can to help you all take down the two remaining families and then go after the Bratva. I have one condition though." They both eye me warily for a moment before Bishop speaks.

"And that is?"

"Anya is innocent and had nothing to do with anything. She isn't to be harmed." Bishop narrows his dark gaze on me, the guys fucking tall and built like superman.

"I'll keep your little friend out of it but hear me, Katarina. You fuck with my brother, I will take your punishment out on her and your brother." I grind my teeth together in anger. King hands me a laptop. I eye it not wanting to take it in case it's a trap.

"Luka programmed it so it's all set up for you to watch him fight from here. I know he won't let you come." I snort out my annoyance which causes him to chuckle lightly. "Don't be mad at him, he just doesn't want you or the...

babies to get hurt." I nod my head in understanding. King's gaze hardens and I steal my spine waiting for him to lash out. "He has spent the past few years hiding in the shadows. He has hated himself for years because of Christine."

"Yeah, well, she's a cunt and lucky she's already dead." Both Bishop and King fight their smiles from breaking free at my words.

"Regardless, it's been years since I have seen my brother without a haunted look in his eyes and that's all thanks to you. We all tried, even Rook tried to bring him back from wallowing in the darkness, but nothing we did worked." I smile at King and shake my head. He doesn't get it.

"That's why he's my dark Knight."

Chapter Thirty-One

Knight

After Bishop dropped, me, Mav, Gage and a few of the other guys off here at Chop's, I went straight to the locker room. Gage and Mav are with me now as I get ready. Neither of us have said a word, we're all lost in our own heads. If everything goes right tonight, we only have Vinny to take out and then we're done. I need this fight. I need the release it will offer me. I'm so fucked up in the head over trying to find my brother, and every day my hope dwindles little by little when I find fucking nothing!

The plan is for each of us to run a part of the city. Bish, King and I all have our parts mapped out. Rook was next and then... who the fuck is the last? Gage isn't a Murdoch so then that must mean it will go to Car?

"Let's strap those hands, get this fight done and get you home." I quirk a brow at Gage in question. "You won't be staying for the final, brother, you have too much to lose now. Mav and I will... finish things after the fight." What he means is, he and Mav will be the ones to put a bullet in AJ's head.

"I'm no pussy," I grit out.

"Never said you were. Shit is happening that you don't know about. This place is packed for a reason. You win the fight, then you get the fuck out, Knight. You don't stick around. Go home to your girl, brother." I slick my eyes between his. I can see unease but there is something else lurking in the depths of his gaze, but I can't pinpoint what it is exactly. Gage flicks his gaze to Mav and then back to me, my eyes widen.

No fucking way!

Gage gives me a subtle nod urging me to remain silent as he continues to tape my hands. Once he's finished, he runs me through a few warm ups. I'm ready to fuck shit up. The announcers call out for the main event. I follow Gage and Mav out, ready to get in the ring and find out who my opponent is. I look around the crowded bar trying to spot AJ. When I can't find him, I peer over my shoulder and shake my head at Gage and Mav. I watch as they both stalk off to go in search of him. The crowd begins to shout and scream, drawing my attention back to the center of the ring. I hide my shock when I watch a shirtless AJ jump into the ring with his hands in the air.

"Fuck," I mutter. His eyes bore into me with a wicked smirk on his face, something is wrong. He shouldn't be in the ring. I was supposed to be fighting the winner of last week's match not him, which means we have a fucking rat in our midst and I'm starting to wonder if Gage's speculations about Mav are true. I try to spot Gage in the crowd but I can't find him. He needs to warn Bishop and King.

The announcer gives his spiel then motions for AJ and me to move into the center. I keep a blank expression on my face as I knock my fists against his. I grit my teeth as I feel the metal beneath his tap. The fucker his brass knuckles on underneath his taped hands.

The bell sounds. We circle each other for a few seconds before he goes on the attack. I dodge left and right trying to find an opening. He fakes right and I shift, big mistake. He lands a solid hit to my ribs. I hiss out in pain, then ignore the searing pain in my side. He manages to land blow after blow with me only managing to land a hit here and there. I need to take this fucker out before he fucking ends me. That's the thing with fighting here, there are no rules. It's kill or be killed and the look in AJ's eyes tells me there is only one of us leaving this ring tonight.

AJ rushes me again. I allow him to get close and then at the last second sweep my leg out and land a decent blow to the side of his head. He stumbles back a few steps, but I don't give him a chance to right himself. I tackle him to the ground and straddle him as I land hit after hit to his ribs and face. Just when I think I have the upper hand, he swings out and lands a right hook to my temple that has black spots dancing in my vision. Another hit comes to my jaw and I flop to the side. The crowd around us screams for blood. He rolls me from my side to my back and resumes the same position I was just in.

I try to lift my arms to shield my face from his assault

but the fucker shifts forward and pins my arms beneath his knees. He smirks down at me before he lifts his fist and slams it into the side of my face. I feel the crack and know the fucker has shattered my cheekbone. Blow after blow lands and I feel myself begin to lose consciousness. I welcome to blackness passing out will offer, at least then I won't be able to feel the final blow that kills me. I'm just about to surrender when suddenly the blows stop. The crowd around us is quiet, then I hear the distinct sound of a gun cocking. My right eye is swollen shut, so I crack my left one open as far as I can and everything inside me locks up as all the air in my lungs flees me. AJ raises his hands slowly whilst keeping his gaze on me. I turn from him to look up and find a pair of bright green eyes looking down at me with an unhinged look.

"You'll pay for this, girl——"

"You touched what is mine and you will pay for that," she sneers.

"I'll kill you," he grits out. She bends down so her lips are in line with his ear, but she keeps her eyes on me the whole time.

"My name is Katarina Antonov, and I'm already dead." His eyes widen in surprise. She stands and pulls the trigger. Blood and brain matter spray all over my face before AJ's dead body flops down onto me. Nathan and Cody are by Koby's side in a second pushing the dead fucker off me and helping me to my feet. Koby pushes Nathan out of the way and wraps my arm around her shoulders. A groan escapes me before I can stop it. She pins me with a disapproving scowl as we make our way to the edge of the ring. I look around and that's when I see my brothers standing near the entrance and all our guys are stationed around the ring with their guns pointed.

Nathan and Cody help me from the ring, then Koby is back at my side helping me toward my brothers. I can feel everyone's gaze on me but I ignore them as I focus on putting one foot in front of the other and ignoring the pain I'm in. Everything inside me fucking aches. If it wasn't for the girl beside me, I would be feeling nothing right now except for dead. As we draw near, Gage steps forward and takes Cody's place on my other side. We walk past Bishop and King, leaving them to deal with the aftermath that will ensue because of what Koby has done.

No one has a single word the whole ride. Gage, Koby and I left before Bish and King. We pull into the driveway and come to a stop at the bottom of the stairs. I sigh when I see Kiara and Ally sitting there waiting for us. I push my door open to climb out, but Gage is there waiting to help me. I eye him for a beat before nodding. He grips my arm and wraps it around his shoulders before wrapping an arm around my waist and leading me past the girls to head inside.

"What the fuck happened?" Kiara demands from behind us.

"Bishop and the others will be here in a few, he can fill you in," Gage calls out without stopping. Once inside he leads me to the living room and helps me sit. I groan as I lay my head back against the couch. "You look like shit." I snort at Gage's attempt to lighten the mood.

"I feel like it," I say as I close my eyes and try to breathe through the pain. My ribs are burning, my kidneys are fucking sore, and my head feels like there is a jackhammer going off inside it. I can barely see out of my left eye—I think my fucking nose is broken as well. I know for sure my cheek is broken or fractured. I feel exhaustion weighing on me and I'm about to give into it when the sound of raised voices in the entryway garners my attention. I don't even bother to open my eye when they shout my name.

Chapter Thirty-Two

Koby

"What the fuck were you thinking?" Bishop shouts right in my face. I don't cower. I stand my ground and hold his judgmental gaze as I reply.

"I was thinking I was saving your brother's fucking life!" He scrubs a hand down his face, then rips his tie from around his neck. Kiara steps in front of him to try calm him but he isn't having any of it. His gaze spears me.

"They want you as payment and Knight is going to fucking kill them for that! I don't need another fucking war, Koby!" he shouts.

"Knight!" King shouts but I ignore him, focusing only on Bishop.

"Then I'll kill them all. I'm not like the others, Bishop. I can hold my fucking own!" I shout back. He slams his eyes closed and drops his head back taking in a few calming breaths to try reign in his temper.

"It was you, wasn't it?" I swing my gaze to King. Whatever he sees in my gaze has his eyes widening. "You were the one that alerted us to the trap, you hacked their building?" I bite my lip and nod.

"How did you know? Luka couldn't get access and he is the fucking best we have." I can hear the anger in Bishop's tone but he isn't angry at me, he's pissed they were caught off guard.

"It was simple. Once I saw it empty, I knew it had to be rigged to blow. King gave me the feed of Knight's fight and when I saw AJ jump into the ring, I knew something was wrong. I sent you both an SOS."

"How did you get there?" King asks. I dart my gaze to Allison, who is looking at her shoes. King rolls his eyes and groans. Ally throws her hands in the air and pins her fiancé with a don't you start look.

"When she explained it to us, I knew it was bad and she said Knight needed her, so I gave her the keys to your car!" Bishop looks to King, they both share a loaded look. I decide to extend an olive branch of sorts and try to help in the only way I know how.

"I hacked your hacker and he's been blocked by someone else." Both guys pin me with a look but I push on before they can interrupt me. "I believe you have a snitch in your midst. Luka is good but he's been blocked and I'm not sure if it's because he isn't as good as you think or he is the snitch." Bishop moves to close the space between us but then Gage is there to push him back a step. They stand chest to chest with their gazes locked in a dick measuring contest.

"Back the fuck off," Bishop snarls.

"I will, but we need the doctor for Knight. He's passed out and had a few blows to the head." Bishop curses and then pulls his phone from his pocket to call the doc. Gage shoots me a look over his shoulder, and I nod my thanks. He did that to save me from wearing the brunt of Bishop's anger.

***

I've been up all night watching Knight. The doc patched him up and said he has a fractured cheek bone and bruised ribs. He re-set his broken nose and put some butterfly stitches on his face. He looks like shit but at least he isn't dead. I know I fucked up last night but I couldn't stand by and watch him die. Bishop has a rat in his organization and he needs to find out who it is before someone does die next time. I startle when a cup of coffee is placed in front of me. Frowning, I look up to see Bishop standing above me.

"I can't—"

"It's decaf." I nod my thanks and grip the cup between my hands as Bishop sits on the other single seater, with his gaze on his brother who is still asleep on the couch. "You saved his life." I don't bother to answer him, there's no point. The silence stretches between us a for a while before he speaks again. "Do you love him?" I keep my gaze on Knight as I answer.

"I wouldn't have outed myself to a room full of connected people if I didn't." I watch him nod from the corner of my eyes, the sun is slowly rising and with that the others will too.

"Dimitri will leave for school next week." That gets my attention. I search his eyes for an ulterior motive but find... none. "He'll have a guard with him always. He will board there and have the best tutors to help him."

"Why are you doing this?" A ghost of a smile touches his lips as he looks to his little brother.

"He has never asked me for a thing his whole life. Within the space of a few months he has asked me for two things."

"And they are?" I hedge. He turns his brown eyes back to me, I stifle my gasp when I see respect in his eyes.

"To not kill you and help your brother." My eyebrows jump up into my hairline in shock. He smiles and for the first time I see it's genuine. "I would have killed you the night you came here with Allison. I would have, if it wasn't for Knight." That shocks the shit out of me, I had no idea. "I think even then he knew you weren't our enemy." I bite the inside of my cheek to keep the tears from rising, fucking hormones. "He'll love you with everything he has inside him, Koby. He'll fuck up, but I promise you, he will never make the same mistake twice."

"Why are you telling me this?" I whisper.

"Because, I once told you I would never trust you and at the time I meant it. It seems I may have been... wrong." My eyes widen and his narrow in warning, earning a light chuckle from me. "I have a proposition for you?" The hairs on the back of my neck rise.

"If you are gonna ask me to leave you can get—"

"No, I would never ask that."

"Okay, what is it then?" The carefree expression he wore moments ago vanishes and is replaced by a stern *don't fuck with me* look.

"Hack for me, help me take down the last two families and take down the Bratva. I give you my word once that is done, you will never have to look over your shoulder or ever have to worry about the safety of your children again." I eye him warily for a moment. He is putting a lot of trust in someone he just admitted he wanted to kill. "You won't accompany us on missions or even leave the confines of this house."

I balk at him. "What the fuck?" I grit out.

"He won't allow it, Koby. You're pregnant with the next generation of Murdoch's and I will not risk their safety for my own gain. If you don't agree, I'll lock your ass in the bunker myself and deal with the bitch fit he'll throw," he says, flicking his head toward Knight. I mull over his words for a moment and really think on what he has asked before I answer him.

"Dimitri is never to be harmed no matter what happens to me." He nods. "I'll stay here and do as you asked but if at any point in time Knight's life is risked and I can prevent it, I will go to him." He nods stiffly. "I'll hack for you *if* you allow Knight to do it with me. He is really good and I can teach him things so he can do better at hiding his tracks and not be sloppy—"

"I'm not fucking sloppy." I gasp. Both Bishop and I turn to Knight and watch as he slowly tries to sit up. Bish rushes over to help him. I smile at him, he is battered and bruised but he still looks fucking sexy as sin. He shoots me a one sided grin that has heat swirling in my belly. He really is my dark Knight.

Chapter Thirty-Three

Knight

I look away from my laptop to smile at Koby. She's in the pool, with the girls and Mela, looking like an absolute fucking snack in that white two-piece bathing suit. She has a small bump now and it fucking does things to me whenever ever I see her sitting on the couch rubbing it or even talking about the future with our kids. She doesn't want to know the sex when the time comes, but I fucking want to know! Bishop agrees that if we have another two girls to add to the family we need to move out to the sticks where they can't sneak out when they are older. Like fuck will my daughters be out partying where disgusting boys can touch them!

"Find anything?" I look over to see King drop into the sun lounger beside me. I close the lid of my laptop and shake my head. It's been weeks since Rook went missing and I can't find a single fucking thing on him, not a glimpse in a video or anything. I have been tracking every fuckers' phone and still I can't find a picture or anything with him in it. I refuse to believe that he is gone. He can't be. He has to be here for the birth of my kids and the day I decide to marry Koby he has to be by my side.

"I won't give up on him," I say sternly. King reaches over and places his hand on top of my shoulder giving it a gentle squeeze.

"None of us will, brother, but there is something you need to do, Knight." I blow out a breath and nod. I know what it is before he even voices it. "She needs to come home before the war starts. Bring her home, brother." I nod and stand. Koby shoots me a worried look. I shake my head and stalk off to call my sister. Carlina is a firecracker. She has the famous Italian temper, truthfully she is probably more ruthless than all of us.

I head around to the front of the house and drop down on the steps, then scroll through my contacts until I find her number. My finger hovers over her name for a minute... As soon as I call her, she'll rush back here. She finally got out and now, I'm about to drag my sister back into this fucked up world we live in.

"She's a big girl, playboy." I turn to the side and smirk. Koby walks toward me with a towel wrapped around her waist and a sexy fucking look in her eyes. "Don't look at me like that, or you won't be making that call." I laugh as she drops down beside me. She's been a lot less on edge now since Dimitri has gone away to school where we used to go. She's happier knowing that her brother has a chance at a normal life, a life she never had the chance to have. "Call her." I nod and finally hit dial before bringing the phone to my ear. Koby rests her head on my shoulder, offering her silent support. The phone rings five times and I'm about to hang when she finally answers.

"Knight," she breathes my name like it's a balm to her soul and it crushes me inside.

"Hey Car." We are both silent for a moment. Koby reaches up and places her hand on my leg, giving it a gentle squeeze. I wrap my arms around her shoulders and pull her in closer.

"How did you find me?" I smirk proudly. She changed her number, but Koby tracked her down a few days ago and got the number to her new cell. She's been traveling through South America since she took off.

"There's a lot to fill you in on but first, I need you to come home." She sighs on the other end of the line making me feel like shit.

"I was wondering how long it would take before one of you guys came calling. Truthfully, I expected you lot to get Rook to guilt me into coming back willingly." A whoosh of air escapes me. I slam my eyes closed trying to garner the strength to tell her the truth. Koby wraps her arms around my waist nuzzling into me further, she knows this is fucking hard for me to say aloud but I have to be the one to do it, he is my twin.

"Car...Rook is..."

"What the fuck is going on, Knight. Where is he?" The concern in her voice is felt all the way to my bones.

"There was an... accident and he——"

"Don't fucking say it!" she pleads, the watery tone of her voice lets me know she is close to tears. I take a deep breath and push myself to get it out.

"He's missing, we need you to come home now. We're at war and Bishop won't make a move until we know you are here safe." She takes a deep breath. I picture her with a scowl on her face and her little nose scrunched up in anger.

"I'll be back as soon as I can." I nod even though she can't see me. "Knight?"

"Yeah?"

"I want to know everything when I get back, don't water shit down for me." I smile. My sister is a fucking force and I pity the guy that ends up with her.

"Deal. When you're back I want an explanation about how you knew about Koby and Dimitri." She's silent for a beat and worry begins to gnaw at me.

"Okay, just... promise to keep an open mind." I grit my teeth then take a deep breath before speaking.

"Okay." We end the call with Car promising to get back here within the week, apparently she has some shit to sort wherever she is before she can come home.

***

Later that evening...

"Well if you had asked me months ago what I saw myself doing in the new year, this sure as fuck wouldn't have been it." Bishop, Gage and I all laugh at King. We're standing around the counter watching our girls and Mela play Uno. It's such a normal thing to do but to us it's... weird. None of us know how to play any board games as we were never allowed to play as kids. I take a sip of my beer and smile wide when Koby throws her head back and laughs at something Ally said. The three of them cut a glance at us and then giggle before huddling their heads together and talking low enough that we can't hear.

"I feel like they are planning something," I say. Bish snorts.

"When aren't they?" That earns a chuckle from all of us.

"You know they are all having a dick measuring contest, right?" The three of us turn to stare at Gage. He shrugs his shoulders like we're fucking dumb for not knowing that.

"Why the fuck would they care, they don't have dicks?" Bishop quips earning a smirk from Gage. "Spit it out dick, what the fuck do you know?" Bishop hates not knowing shit. He and Kiara have a deal, they can't lie to each other, so the thought of her hiding something from him has him on edge.

"They aren't talking about themselves, asshole. They're talking about *your* dicks." Bishop puffs his chest out like he's won the contest. King and I both snort at the cocky fucker.

"We all know I was named *King* for a reason." Bishop pins him a disgusted look.

"Your pin dick is nothing compared to mine!" I step in wanting to put an end to this bickering.

"You're both wrong, I have the biggest cock out of all of you." They both gape at me but my victory is short lived when all three girls turn again but this time their gazes are on... Gage. We all follow their line of sight and pin him with a glare.

"What?" he snaps, looking between us, then it dawns on me. I throw my head back laughing. I can feel their angry stares on me so I clamp my mouth shut and pat Bish and King on the back and fill them in on what I know.

"All three of those girls have seen our cocks." Both of them nod but I can see they are both confused as hell still. "Only *one* of them has seen Gage's..." I let my sentence trail, allowing them time to come to their own conclusion. Gage's eyes widen and smartly rounds the corner away from Bishop who a second later pins him with a look that promises pain.

"I'm gonna fucking end you," Bish growls out, before stomping into the living room, gripping Kiara around the waist and hauling her over his shoulder caveman style, causing everyone to laugh at his brooding possessive ass. I make my way to my girl and offer my hand, she takes it willingly and steps into my arms wrapping her own around my waist.

"You told them I was the biggest, right?" Ally and Koby both laugh. I hear King and Gage muttering shit behind me but ignore them. For the first time in a long time I feel at peace within myself. There is a part of me that knows I will never be whole again though. My soul was ripped in half the night my brother disappeared, that piece of me will never heal. I'll live with that void inside myself for as long as I shall live.

Epilogue

Bishop

Four days later...

I pace the length of my office needing something to do other than sitting in my fucking chair waiting. Carlina was supposed to have been here hours ago. I sent Mav and Luka to collect her from the airport but she never made it off the flight. They scoured the whole fucking airport and came up empty. Knight and Koby sit on the couch in my office with their faces buried in their computers. King is out searching for her, I know there is no way she could have been intercepted by Pauly or Vinny. We've been tracking them since the night of the fight. I feel Kiara's gaze on me but I can't let her distract me, I need to think.

"Uh." I stop pacing and turn to Koby who looks like she is ready to puke, it's all she fucking does these days. The smell of coffee, food or any fucking thing makes her throw up. Kiara thinks I'm an ass because I don't pity her, but fuck it, she isn't my girl to care for.

"You need to take a break, baby?" Knight asks. It's still a shocking sight for me to witness. The change in my brother was almost instant, as soon as he stopped fighting his feelings for her it was like a side of him he had buried came back to life.

"No, but I think you should see this." Knight looks to me and I make my way over. Kiara rushes to my side and I pull her in front of me wrapping my arms around her middle and resting my chin on her shoulder. Koby looks to Knight and I can tell from the frown on his face he can tell something isn't right.

"Just say it, baby." She nods and pulls up a picture. Kiara gasps and I stiffen behind her, Knight curses.

"Is that..." Kiara can't even bring herself to say the words.

"That is Vincent Murelo, Vinny Murelo's son," Koby says, barely above a whisper. I stare at the picture unsure of what the fuck to do, the time stamp on the photo reads two days ago. In the picture Carlina is walking hand in hand through the airport with our enemies fucking son! She has no fucking idea that she is in danger or that his father had a hand in our brother's death.

"Find her now and fucking bring me that cock sucker's head. I want our sister back in this fucking house before the day is out!" I growl. Knight nods his agreement, he's ready to take out his vengeance on the fucker. He'll pay for the crimes of his father, that I can promise you.

"Bishop?" I cut my gaze to Koby and nod for her to continue. "I've searched him before, Vincent. He doesn't come up on any database on the web at all."

"What are you saying?" I snap, earning a glare from my brother.

"I done some digging, Vincent Murelo is supposed to be dead. That guy may look like him but he isn't Vinny's son." I furrow my brow in confusion.

"Then who the fuck is he?" I ask, knowing she has the answer.

"From what I found, he is known as the Bloodhound. He's who people use to sniff out their enemies. He has a kill rate of 100%. He is a hired killer, Bishop. That guy is the one you send in when everything else fails. I think your sister is in real danger here."

Click the link to read Carlina's story,
Tempted By The Queen

Condemned Beast

Secret Society/ Bully

Filthy Few

Forever Filthy

Filthiest Of Them All

Masked Men Novella (Pure Smut)

Dirty Priest

Dirty Daddy

Sports Romance

Playing For Keeps

Offside

Touchdown

End Game

Hail Mary

Blindside

RH Sports

Hate Us Like You Mean It

MM

Love Me Like You Mean It

Paranormal Romance

The Veil Of Obsidian

Of Time And Carnage

Curse Of Fate

Dream

Fate

Nightmare

Redemption

Anarchy

<u>Brutal Savages</u>

Savage Lies

Brutal Truth

Savage Beast

Brutal Beauty

ACKNOWLEDGMENT

My girl Tash, thank you for helping me plot out this whole series and listening to me cry about how much I wanted to stop because everyone would hate these guys. Funny right? Thank you heaps babe for being there for me.

My amazing editor Liz, thank you so much for all your hard work and loving these guys as much as I do. You make all these book babies so pretty and perfect.

My ARC team, thank you ladies for reading these books and helping me polish them before they go live. These books wouldn't be what they are without you.

My baby daddy, you are a DILF and I love riding that D nightly baby!

My babies, you both give me the inspiration I need to kill off and harm these characters lol Love you both.

My readers, without you all none of this would be possible so thank you. Thank you for reading these books and loving my guys as much as I do.

Sam
Xxx